WAGGIT AGAIN

ALSO BY PETER HOWE

Waggit's Tale

To Franklin School

Peter Howe

PETER HOWE

WAGGIT AGAIN

Drawings by
Omar Rayyan

HarperCollins*Publishers*

Library of Congress Cataloging-in-Publication Data is available.

Howe, Peter, 1942-

Waggit again / by Peter Howe ; interior illustrations by Omar

Rayyan. — 1st ed.

p. cm.

Summary: After being left in the country by his owner, Waggit sets

out on the long journey to New York City and meets some unexpected

friends along the way.

ISBN 978-0-06-124264-9 (trade bdg.) — ISBN 978-0-06-124265-6

(lib bdg.)

[1. Dogs—Fiction.] I. Rayyan, Omar, ill. II. Title.

PZ7.H8377Wad 2009   2008020213

[Fic]—dc22   CIP

                                                                     AC

Typography by Amy Ryan

09 10 11 12 13 LP/RRDB 10 9 8 7 6 5 4 3 2 1

❖

First Edition

*This book is dedicated to working dogs everywhere
and especially to the memory of my wonderful
therapy dog Bobby Blue, who brought so much joy
to so many children in distress.*

TABLE OF CONTENTS

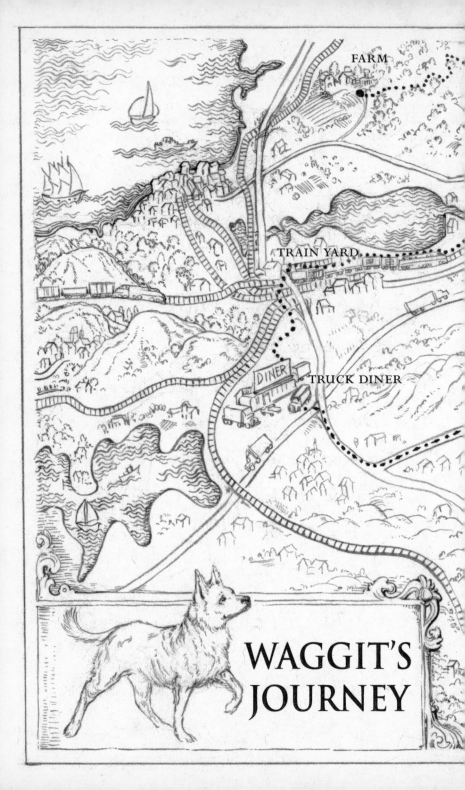

FARM

TRAIN YARD

DINER

TRUCK DINER

WAGGIT'S
JOURNEY

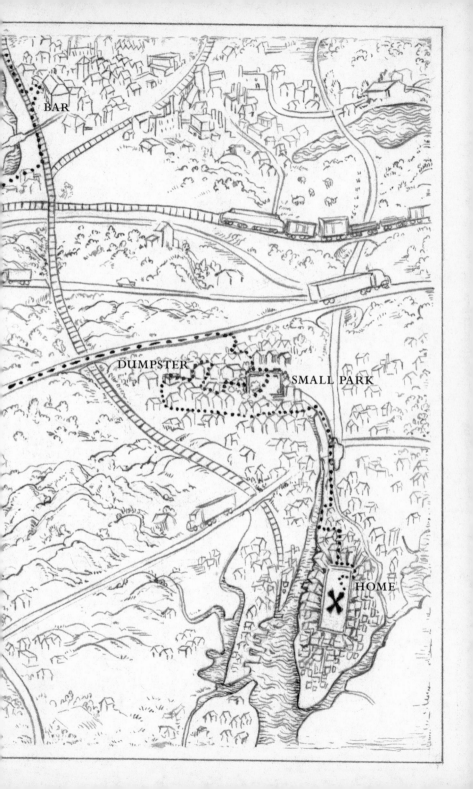

1

Waggit's Escape

Even though he was wearing his leather collar Waggit could still feel the chain biting into his neck as he pulled on it. It hurt to move the links backward and forward over the sharp edge of the rock, but he could bear the pain; what he couldn't tolerate was staying one more day on this farm. So he had done the same thing every night for weeks, ever since the farmer staked him out in the backyard after his fight with the dog called Hodge. The chain was old and rusty, but so far it had resisted his best efforts to snap it.

Maybe tonight, he thought. Maybe it will break tonight.

The night was moonless and very dark, and his escape would be that much easier if he broke free now. He continued to pace back and forth, keeping the chain taut, his head held down, listening to the grinding noise of the metal as it chafed against the rock. The task was made more difficult by the need for silence. The other dogs slept unshackled only a few feet away, and any of them, Hodge in particular, would have raised the alarm if they heard his attempts to break free.

Hodge was the leader of the farmyard dogs. His name was short for Hodgepodge, and he was a tough, lumbering creature who looked as if he had been made out of the parts left over from other dogs. When Waggit and his owner had arrived at the farm after a long drive, she had let him loose in the yard. He had been pleased to see other dogs and had run up to them eagerly. To his surprise they all cowered as he came near. He was just about to explain that he only wanted to say hello when he heard a growl behind him. He turned to see Hodge, his teeth bared and his hackles up.

"Well, what do we have here?" the tough dog said with contempt. "Is this a city dog I see? Have you come here to teach us all your fancy city ways?"

"No," said Waggit, not sure why the dog was being so aggressive. "I only wanted to say hi. I'm just visiting. My owner's going to take me back home in a minute."

"Well," said Hodge, "you'd better hope she does, 'cause we've got some country ways *we* can teach *you*, and they all involve pain."

But as it turned out, Waggit's owner didn't take him back. She had driven off, and although at first he had confidently waited for her to return and take him to the city, his optimism had drained away as many days passed and still there was no sign of her. He became resigned to life in the yard, keeping to himself, which wasn't hard to do. If any of the other dogs approached him or tried to be friendly, Hodge snarled at them and told them to leave the "city boy" alone.

This went on until Waggit could stand it no longer. The farmer fed the dogs once a day, putting down battered metal bowls that contained mostly table scraps. Hodge would frequently wolf down his own food and then shove another dog out of the way and take his or her meal as well. He had never tried it with Waggit until one day.

Waggit was about to put his nose into his bowl when he was knocked sideways by Hodge's shoulder.

"Leave it," Waggit barked as the bully was about to empty the bowl of its contents.

"Oh my, a tough guy," Hodge sneered. "And we were all of us just saying what a scaredy-cat you seem to be."

Now, you can call a dog any number of nasty things and they will roll right off his back, but only the most timid of dogs would tolerate being called a scaredy-cat—and Waggit was far from timid. Hodge didn't realize that even though Waggit was still young, he hadn't always been the spoiled pet the country dog mistook him for. Parts of Waggit's short life had been very hard indeed, and although not a fighter by nature, he could only be pushed so far.

Waggit leapt at Hodge without warning, taking the other dog by surprise and putting him on his back. Hodge quickly recovered and went on the attack. But if he was much stronger, Waggit was much quicker, and he would dart in and nip the bigger dog and then retreat. As his opponent lumbered toward him he continued his hit-and-run tactics, driving the bigger dog wild. How this would have ended nobody will ever know, because the noise that the other dogs made as they watched—plus the angry growls of Hodge as he grew more and more frustrated—attracted the farmer's attention, and the next thing Waggit knew he was chained up. The farmer didn't care who was right and who was wrong; he simply needed peace in the farmyard.

Waggit was happy to oblige the man by removing himself completely. And so he moved backward and forward, backward and forward, knowing that every scrape of metal against stone brought him a little closer to freedom. His neck ached with the effort, but still the link wouldn't give. He took a short break and noticed that the sky was beginning to get a little lighter. Dawn was coming. The thought of another day on the farm so panicked him that he pulled against the chain with all his might. Suddenly there was a ping and he fell backward. The chain had broken! Unfortunately as it snapped it snaked back across the yard and hit the sleeping Hodge squarely on the nose. He yelped and sat up, instantly awake.

Hodge immediately understood what was happening and raced across the yard barking, causing all the other dogs to bark as well. The area was completely fenced in, but Waggit had already planned how he was going to get out; now he had to do it as quickly as possible. He had one handicap, however. Although he was free of most of the chain, about two feet of it still hung around his neck. Picking the trailing end up in his mouth, he sprinted to the corner of the yard where bags of fertilizer were stacked on wooden pallets and leapt from a run onto the top of the stack. Although the chain wasn't heavy, it was cumbersome, and he barely made it, digging his claws into the plastic sacks, his heart in his mouth along with the chain.

He paused for breath while Hodge and two of the other dogs barked ferociously at the foot of the pile, leaping up, desperately trying to get to him but lacking the agility to do so. Waggit saw a light go on in the farmer's bedroom and knew that he didn't have much time. The jump over the fence was not a problem, not more than a couple of feet. It was the drop to the ground on the other side that was intimidating, for there was nothing to break his fall. He worried that the chain might get caught on the fence as he went over it, leaving him hanging by the neck.

In the end he had no alternative but to jump, sailing over the fence as if he were flying until gravity took over and brought him crashing to the ground. Pain shot through his legs and the wind left his body as he hit the hard earth. When he got his breath back he scrambled to his feet, shook himself, checked that he was okay, and then ran as fast as he could, leaving the three dogs clawing at the fence, snarling and cursing at him. The last thing he heard from the farmyard was the voice of the farmer yelling, "Be quiet, you dogs. What's going on?"

2
An Unusual Upright

Waggit ran and ran until he could run no more and had to lie down in some bushes, panting as if he would never stop. He was pretty sure that he was far enough away now, so even if the farmer did come looking for him the man would be unlikely to find him. But although he was feeling safe, he was also feeling lost. He had no idea where he was or which way he should go. Whichever direction he took, he would have to be careful. Although dogs alone on country roads might be a more familiar sight than in the city, those with two feet of chain attached to their collars would attract unwanted attention.

He got up from the bushes and stretched. He had found that stretching was a good thing to do when you had to make a decision; it seemed to make thinking easier. He sniffed the air as if trying to pick up some scent of the city. He knew this was silly and that his home was many miles from here, but even so he felt a tingling in his nostrils when he faced in a certain direction, not a smell exactly but a sort of feeling. His whiskers also twitched like a water diviner's rod. He turned around in a full circle several times, but the sensation only happened when he was facing one particular way. Since he had nothing else to guide him he decided to follow this instinct and headed down the road in that direction.

In the distance he heard the sound of a truck snorting as it applied its brakes and rounded a bend. Waggit quickly jumped into the ditch on the side of the road and lay as flat as possible until the vehicle, a large milk tanker, passed him by. The sky was quite light now, and it would be safer if he could find a route that wasn't a highway. More and more cars were about, and soon he was spending as much time hiding in the ditch as walking.

He had gone several miles and was beginning to feel tired and hungry when he came upon a lane that went away from the highway and into the fields. It was deeply rutted where tractors or trucks had used it, and it looked interesting to the dog. On either side stone walls and thick, prickly bushes hid him from sight; it seemed a better alternative than the road. He was still too scared to relax though, and he moved quickly along, glancing over his shoulder every few feet to make sure that he wasn't being followed. He had gone only a short distance when his heart sank. The path ended at a metal gate that led into an empty field from which there appeared to be no exit.

But then something at the far end of the field caught his attention. It was a tall, grassy embankment, on top of which he could see poles with wires strung between them. Something about the embankment aroused his curiosity and he squeezed his body under the bottom of the closed gate and headed toward it. He quickly ran across the field and scampered up the side of the ridge.

When he came to the top he was on a flat surface covered in small rocks, over which ran two strips of metal that were mounted at intervals on crosspieces of wood and seemed to go on forever. Waggit had no idea what all this was for—he had never seen a railroad— but he could see it was free of cars, trucks, and people. His nose told him it was heading in the right direction. Taking it, however, was easier said than done. The rocks hurt his feet, and the wooden planks were spaced too far apart for comfort. He tried walking beside the tracks, but the slope was too steep and it tired him. The best he could do was stay between the rails, and after a while he got into a rhythm alternating between rocks and planks that made it bearable.

Apart from the surface, the railroad tracks were perfect. They went through deep countryside, and not only did he see no people, he rarely saw houses, and when he did they were far in the distance. The sun had been up for some time and was warm without being hot. Birds were singing in the trees, and he smelled a hint of cherry blossoms. He felt so lighthearted that he even dropped the chain from his mouth and let it jingle musically on the ground. Although he was fearsomely hungry, at least he wasn't thirsty. The tracks had gone through a deep cutting in the rock, with sheer sides rising up many feet. From a crack in the walls a small waterfall descended, and under this Waggit quenched his thirst and cooled his body.

His feeling of contentment was short-lived, however. No more than a mile from the cutting, the tracks ran through more open countryside. Suddenly he felt the earth beneath his paws begin to vibrate, gently at first, and then more noticeably. His ears picked up the sound of rumbling, not the kind that trucks made but much different. Then he heard the shriek of a whistle, and as he turned and looked behind him he saw a terrible sight. An awesome metal monster was bearing down upon him, its single headlight glaring like a huge, malevolent eye, angry black fumes coming out of its nostrils.

Waggit just had time to throw himself down the embankment before the beast was upon him. It roared past, an unstoppable force, dragging dozens of large metal boxes behind it. These were freight cars that clattered rhythmically over the joins in the rails, sounding like they were saying, "Gotta go, gotta go, gotta go." The train appeared to be endless, and Waggit feared he would never be able to walk along the tracks again, but finally, after what seemed like hours, the last car passed. Silence once again descended on the landscape, although the dog couldn't tell because the sound the locomotive had made was so loud that his ears were still ringing.

"Well, young man, who are you and where are you going?"

Waggit spun around to see a woman standing behind him, not young but not really old either. He hadn't heard her come up because of the noise reverberating in his head. She was dressed in an assortment of strange, mismatched clothes. She had a scarf tied under her chin with an old and ragged baseball cap on top of it. Across her shoulders she wore a cape, now faded to a pale blue but still trimmed in red. Beneath it was a thick woolen plaid shirt of the kind that people think lumberjacks wear. She had on a flowing skirt that came below her knees with black sweatpants under it, and on her feet were a rugged pair of work boots. The entire outfit should have looked ridiculous, but the way she carried herself gave it a stylish quality.

Waggit's first instinct was to back off and put up his hackles, but there was something about her that was strangely soothing, and he realized that he didn't fear her at all. He wasn't sure why; it might have been the sound of her voice, which was musical and calming, but it was more than that. Just being near her made him feel peaceful. He cocked his head and looked at her. Then he realized she had asked him a question.

"My name is Waggit," he replied, "and I'm trying to go home."

"I'm very pleased to meet you, Waggit," she said in her wonderful voice. "My name is Felicia. Now where exactly is your home?"

"It's where my friends live."

"Hmm." She considered this thoughtfully. "That doesn't give us much of a clue as to whether or not you're going in the right direction."

"Well," he said, "every time I turn this way my nose tingles, so I think it's right."

"Yes," Felicia agreed, "that's always a good sign."

Then something struck Waggit with the force of the train. He understood what she was saying, and she understood him. Not only that, she spoke to him the way dogs talk to each other, without making a sound and without moving her lips. Her words just popped into his brain the way they did with other dogs. This had never happened before with a human being.

"How come you know what I'm saying? I mean, you're an Upright, and Uprights can't understand dogs." He cocked his head in confusion.

"I'm a what?"

"An Upright, you know. You're a people."

"Well, I suppose I am. I just never heard that term before," she said.

"So?" persisted Waggit. "How come?"

"Well, I may be an Upright, but I also have"—she paused for an instant—"shall we say, certain powers that most people don't have, or at least don't think they have."

"That's amazing," said Waggit, truly impressed. "Can you talk to all animals?"

"I don't know," she replied. "I suppose I could if I tried, but I only bother with the ones I like. You dogs are my favorites, with horses second, and I also find pigs quite amusing. Cows are rather dull, and I don't like cats. They're way too full of themselves."

"Do other Uprights who can't talk to their animals ask you to tell them what we're saying?" he inquired.

"Bless you, no," she said with a twinkle of amusement in her eyes, "quite the opposite. They think I'm strange, to put it mildly. To them I'm just a little less threatening than a witch."

Waggit didn't know what a witch was, but the

thought of this calm woman with her soothing voice being a threat to anyone seemed odd to him.

"Come," she said, "you have a 'lean and hungry look' as Mr. Shakespeare said, and I think I have some sausages that we can cook up. Let's go to my place."

Waggit didn't know who Mr. Shakespeare was either, but whoever he was he apparently knew a thing or two about dogs and their digestive systems, because the word *sausage* caused Waggit's stomach to start growling louder than Hodge in a bad mood. He trotted along beside her until they came to a small tent set a little way back from the tracks. She had covered it with leaves and branches so that at first sight it was almost invisible. A narrow, clear stream ran close to the tent, and Waggit ran to it to drink and let the cold water wash over his paws and ease the soreness from walking on the rocks that lay beneath the rails.

When he went back to the campsite Felicia was putting some sticks and dead, dry leaves into a circle of blackened stones. She then disappeared inside the tent, and Waggit could hear her muttering to herself.

"Matches. Matches. Now come on, matches, where are you?"

After a couple of minutes he heard her cry, "Ah-ha!"

and she reemerged, her baseball cap slightly crooked, triumphantly holding a large box of matches in her hand. She busily lit the fire, talking to the matches all the while, encouraging them to do their work. Once she got a good blaze going she let it burn for a while until all that remained of the wood were hot, glowing embers. She placed an old, battered frying pan on the coals, and into this she threw some fat sausages. Soon the sound of sizzling and the delicious smell of meat cooking wafted through the air, causing Waggit to drool.

Felicia noticed this and said, "I know that it doesn't matter to you whether they're cooked or not, but since I live without the benefits of a refrigerator it's probably best that we heat them through. We don't want you getting sick."

Although this was sensible, it was also a nuisance, as many sensible things are. By the time she put the food on a plate and placed the plate on the ground, Waggit thought he would faint from hunger. The actual eating of the sausages was the shortest part of the whole process, and when it was over, and the dog got that wonderful, restful sensation of a full stomach, he belched softly.

"Now that you've eaten," she said as she cleaned out the frying pan with a handful of grass, "let's try to work out where your home is."

She put the pan back into the tent and turned toward him only to find that he was fast asleep, exhausted from the excitement of the day's adventures and the effect of the food.

"Oh well, maybe later," she said kindly.

3

Travel Plans

Waggit awoke to the sensation of being stroked. Felicia was gently smoothing the fur down his back and caressing him behind his ears. She made him feel safe and peaceful, more relaxed than before his owner had left him at the farm.

"Welcome back," she said as he stretched and yawned.

He got up and shook himself, and in doing so realized that she had gently taken off the length of chain while he slept. This was a great relief, because even though it didn't weigh much, it did get in the way and, worse, it was a reminder of his recent captivity. He wagged his tail in gratitude and then sat down again.

"Well," she said, "I think we know where your home is—or at least where it was at one time."

She reached over to his collar and shook the rather battered red tag that hung from it.

"That, my friend, is a rabies vaccination tag from a New York City vet. So we know you lived in New York at one time. Why you don't have any other identification tags I have no idea."

Waggit remembered that in his fight with Hodge some of the stuff that jingled from his collar had been ripped off and fallen to the ground, never to be reattached.

"New York sounds familiar," he said uncertainly.

"Was it a big city with lots of people and very tall buildings?"

He nodded.

"And yellow cabs?" she asked.

"I don't know what a cab is," he admitted.

"You know, a car," she said. "A big metal thing that goes along the road carrying people—er, Uprights, that is—inside."

"Oh, a roller." He finally understood. "There were a lot of rollers that color."

"Assuming that a roller is a car, then we can also assume that the yellow ones were taxis. I think," she said, "that your home is New York, and that you're a long way from it. How did you end up in this neck of the woods?"

"I was living with a woman. She was the one who rescued me from the Great Unknown."

"The Great Unknown? I don't think I've ever heard of that."

"It's where they take you when they catch you in the park," explained Waggit. "Anyway, we lived together for many risings, and everything seemed just fine until one day she suddenly put me in a roller and brought me to a farm near here and left me there."

"Why did she do that?" asked Felicia.

"I don't know." The dog was really confused. "I thought she liked me; she seemed to. I liked her, and I trusted her, but she abandoned me, like the first Uprights I lived with did." He suddenly was shaking with anger. "That's what you get for trusting Uprights. I should've learned my lesson; I promise you I'll never trust another one."

"Whoa, slow down there. I'm an Upright and you trust me, don't you?" said Felicia.

Strangely enough, he did, although he wasn't sure why.

"Also," the woman continued, "there are many reasons to leave a dog somewhere. It doesn't necessarily mean she abandoned you. Maybe she left you there because she had to go away and wanted them to look after you. Maybe she was coming back."

"No," said Waggit. "She never went away for that long. It was too many risings ago. No, she abandoned me."

"Oh dear, you do feel sorry for yourself."

"So would you if you'd been abandoned, for the second time, as it happens."

"No I wouldn't," she cheerfully contradicted him. "I would say to myself: Here's the opportunity to do something different; here's the possibility of an adventure."

"That's easy for you to say," replied Waggit, somewhat resentful of her breezy optimism. "You've probably never been abandoned."

"Actually, I was, in a way." He waited for her to explain what she meant by this, but she fell silent.

"Look," she said after a few minutes, "why don't we do this? I haven't been to New York City in a long time, and it might be fun to see if it's changed. I've nothing special to do at the moment, so why don't I join you and we'll go there together? Sound like a plan?"

It did sound like a plan to Waggit, especially since he didn't have one of his own. Furthermore, she made him feel happy, even if he didn't particularly want to be. He wagged his tail in agreement.

"Good," Felicia exclaimed, "that's settled. Let's shake on it."

She extended her hand, and he put his paw in it. It was a deal. They were traveling companions.

"I think," said Felicia, "that with all due respect to your nose, I shall buy a map at the first opportunity."

They decided that they would start out in the morning, and as the day drew to a close the woman prepared yet another meal. This time she opened cans of beef chili and warmed them in the same pan in which she had cooked the sausages. She put two large dollops of the food on a plate for herself but let Waggit eat his directly from the pan, when it had cooled down. Of course, being chili, even when it had cooled down it was still hot, because that's the way chili is. It surprised the dog, who had never tasted spicy food before, but when he got used to it he found it delicious, and furthermore, as he licked the last remnants from the pan he could still taste the morning's sausages.

While the woman washed out the utensils in the stream before it got totally dark, Waggit lay by the opening of the tent licking his paws. He looked at Felicia as she worked. He had never met a human like her before. It wasn't just that she understood what he said or the peace he felt in her company—both of these things were remarkable enough—but she also didn't seem to have any of the worries and concerns that other humans had. She wasn't always in a hurry, and from the eccentric way that she was dressed she clearly didn't care what other people thought of her. She was so calm and confident that he couldn't imagine her being frightened.

"Are you ever afraid of things?" he asked her when she returned.

"Not often," she replied. "I've found that things are rarely as scary as you think they're going to be. That's the trouble with fear. It holds you back. It stops you from doing things that might be fun or might be good for you. Take this journey we're about to go on. I'm sure we'll come across stuff that won't be what we expect, and some parts of it will be difficult, but if you let fear of what might happen stop you, then you might as well stay right here forever."

Funnily enough Waggit had been thinking that living with Felicia in the tent by the stream was so nice that maybe they shouldn't take the long and possibly hazardous trip back to New York, but he didn't mention this to her.

"I'll give you an example," Felicia continued. "When we get to New York we've got to find where your woman lives. Locating someone in a big city is difficult even if you have a name and address, neither of which is in our possession, and New York is as big as big cities get. But I know that once you start moving forward, things have a tendency to fall into place, and so I have no doubt that it'll work out."

Waggit sat there, stunned.

"But——" he began.

"No," said Felicia. "Not another word. We'll find her if it takes every power that I possess."

"But—" Waggit tried again. "But I don't want to find her."

"You don't?" asked Felicia, puzzled. "I thought you wanted to go home."

"I do," said Waggit. "I do want to go home. I want to go home to the park."

4

Getting Acquainted

It was Felicia's turn to be surprised.

"Hold on there," she said. "Are you telling me that the woman lived in a park?"

"No, no," said Waggit. "The team lived in the park."

It was quite dark now, and the only light was from the glowing embers of the fire and the cold light of the moon. Waggit moved closer to Felicia, and in the darkness he told her the story of his life. He told her that when he was very young, just a puppy, he had been left in the park by a human he had been living with, but had been rescued by a big, black dog called Tazar. Tazar was the leader of a team of dogs that lived there without any humans caring for them. Waggit told Felicia of the friends he had made, especially a short-legged, scruffy dog called Lowdown who was much older than him, and whom he feared might now be dead. He told her how hard it was to survive in the park during the winter but also of the fun they had in the snow and on the frozen lakes. He told her about their enemies, a tough, violent dog called Tashi, and Wilbur, his evil lieutenant. He told her that he owed his life to the team, and that they were really the only family he had.

Then he went on to tell her about meeting the woman. She was a singer by profession, and as the weather got warmer she came to the park to eat her lunch and practice her songs. She had shared her food with him, and it became his routine to be in the same place every day to see her—and one day she wasn't there but a park ranger was. He caught Waggit and took him to the pound. In a very quiet voice he told her about the pound and the door in the wall that they took you through if you were there too long. He told her that nobody ever returned after they went through the door. Then he told her how the woman had come back and rescued him, and how he had decided to stay with her rather than return to his friends. But now he regretted that decision and wanted to rejoin the team, if they would have him, if indeed there still was a team.

Even though Waggit was young, the story of his life was long because so many things had happened to him in such a short time, and some of them were painful to recall. He looked up at Felicia and thought he saw a tear catch in the moonlight as it trickled down her face. She put her hand on his head, and the ache he was feeling in his heart seemed to vanish.

"They'll take you back," she said. "Anyone would. You're such a good dog."

With that reassurance they prepared to sleep. Felicia thought he might be happier spending the night outside, but Waggit welcomed the opportunity to lie next to her and feel her comforting warmth as he cuddled up to the softness of her sleeping bag. He felt safe and snug, and the day had been long and exciting, so it surprised him that he couldn't fall asleep. He thought from her breathing that Felicia was awake as well.

"Felicia."

"Yes, Waggit?"

"Are you awake?"

"I think I must be."

"Can I ask you something?"

"Sure you can."

"How did you learn to talk to dogs? Who taught you?"

"Oh," said Felicia, "that's a long story."

"I'm not going anywhere," said Waggit. "And anyway, I told you about my life. If we're going to travel together I should know about yours."

"That seems reasonable," said Felicia. "Where shall I begin? Well, I'm told that I come from a good family. What it's good for I'm not quite sure, but many generations ago one of my ancestors made a lot of money, and the family's been living off of his hard work ever since, including me. You see," she said, with a twinkle in her eye, "I may be strange, but I'm strange with a trust fund."

Waggit didn't know what that was, but anything with the word *trust* in it was probably good.

"Go on," he said.

Felicia paused for a moment, putting all the events

of her life into order in her mind.

"I grew up," she began, "in a big house in the country, not far from here, actually. I had a very privileged life, with all of the comforts that anyone could wish for: servants to look after me, a chauffeur to drive me, and my own pony to ride. I had everything except friends, and I was lonely. I had no brothers or sisters; I didn't go to school because I had someone who taught me by myself, and my mother and father were hardly ever there. When they were they didn't take much notice of me."

"Did the Upright who taught you tell you how to speak to dogs?" asked Waggit.

"Bless you, no," said Felicia with a chuckle. "She taught me how to speak to French people but not to dogs. No, the woman who did that wouldn't have been allowed inside our house."

"Where did you meet her, then?" asked Waggit.

"The house was surrounded by lots of land, much of it wooded," she continued, "and one day when I was about—oh, I suppose I must have been a teenager—and bored with the activities that had been planned for me, I took a long walk in the woods, farther than I had ever been before. I was just about to turn back when I came upon a hut that someone had built out of dead branches and leaves, more like a shelter, really. Sitting in front of it was this old woman, and we got to talking. She lived every summer in our woods, and nobody knew she was there, not my parents or anyone who worked for them. She didn't own anything, but she knew everything about the woods and the creatures that lived there."

"Did she know about dogs?" asked Waggit.

"She did," said Felicia, "but more to the point, dogs knew about her. I had taken my black lab, Smutty, with me on the walk, and he was the one who found her first. By the time I got up to them they were in the middle of a long conversation, which of course I didn't even know was taking place."

"But she taught you the language, right?" asked Waggit.

"She taught me that if you love creatures and you open your mind and your heart to them, there are no limits to what you can say or feel. All Uprights have the ability, but over the years they've forgotten how to do it because other things became more important to them, like getting ahead and making money and being powerful."

"What happened to her?"

"I went to see her every summer," said Felicia, "and she taught me all she could about trees and plants and animals. This went on for maybe five or six years, and then one summer she told me it would be the last one. She knew she was going to die, but she wasn't sad. She loved nature, and to her death was part of nature, just a part of life really. And she was right. It was the last time I saw her, but after I realized she had gone I decided I wanted to live the way she lived and to value the things she valued. So I became a wanderer. I don't have a huge amount of money but enough to live simply, and I get to go to wonderful places and make fascinating acquaintances like you."

"What about your family?" Waggit asked. "Don't they worry about you?"

"They did at first," said Felicia. "But now they think I'm crazy, and so they leave me alone. There's a certain freedom in people thinking you're mad, you know. Besides, as long as I'm taking money out of the bank from time to time they know I'm alive."

The dog had been fascinated by her story but now he began to feel tired. He tried not to show it, but a yawn came and he couldn't stop it.

"We should get some rest," said Felicia. "We begin our grand adventure tomorrow, and we need to start out full of energy."

So once again they settled down, Felicia in her sleeping bag and Waggit nestled against her, feeling safe and drowsy. Tomorrow would be a big day, and he was both excited and a little scared about what might befall them, but he was happy to have this companion with him on his journey home.

5

The Journey Begins

It rained heavily during the night, but the next morning was bright and fresh, as if the earth's face had been scrubbed clean. Felicia got up early and was cooking bacon when Waggit awoke. In fact it was the delectable aroma that aroused him. It wasn't the only enticing odor, however. Everything was bursting with life, and he could almost smell energy and optimism in the air. It was the scent of spring, and it felt like a good day to start an adventure.

After they had eaten and Felicia had washed herself

in the stream, she started to pack up her belongings. It was amazing how she could get everything into her large backpack. Waggit watched in fascination as she carefully folded each item of clothing and placed all of them in the bottom of the bag. She then put in a layer of plastic sheeting and several layers of newspaper before placing the food on top. When she had completely filled the backpack she zipped it shut and attached the rolled-up tent and sleeping bag. She checked around to make sure that she hadn't left any trash at the campsite, then squatted down and put the pack on her back. She stood up carefully and turned to Waggit.

"The journey of a thousand miles begins with a single step," she said, and strode off.

He had no idea how far a mile was, but a thousand of them sounded like a very long way, and he was hoping that New York was a bit closer. He had no time to worry about this, however, because Felicia was already some distance down the railroad tracks and he had to run to catch up with her. The day was fine and the countryside was beautiful. The stream had now broadened into a shallow river that sparkled in the sun. On a couple of occasions when the two of them had to scramble down the bank to let a train pass, Felicia took off her boots, hoisted up her sweatpants, and let her feet dangle in the clean, flowing water. Waggit waded up to his shoulders, enjoying the cold shock of it against his chest. Lazy brown fish drifted against the current but scattered when he got too close. Waggit was a city dog and had hated the country when he was on the farm. He hated the smells, the isolation, and most of all the silence. He missed the comforting hum of traffic and the constant movement of a great metropolis. But here, cooling himself in the river with his new friend close by, he felt quite comfortable.

Toward the end of the afternoon Waggit's nose started to twitch. He could smell humans, and sure enough, as they rounded a bend in the tracks by a wooded grove they saw a small town in the distance. Felicia decided she would have to go there to get the supplies they needed but that it was too late now and it would be better if they camped in the woods for the night. She found a good spot that was well protected but accessible, and there she pitched the tent.

Immediately after breakfast the next morning Felicia got ready to leave.

"We're running short of several essentials," she said, "including food."

Waggit suddenly felt tense and anxious. Was her trip into the distant town just her way of getting rid of him? No, that couldn't be because she was leaving her tent and most of her belongings; nevertheless he felt uncomfortable.

"We don't need food. There's plenty of food here." He nodded to the woods and fields that surrounded them. "I'm a pretty good hunter, and I can get us a curlytail or a hopper."

Felicia smiled. "While I'm sure that curlytails and hoppers taste delicious, whatever they are, I think I would like to stick to the food I'm used to. Besides, we also need other stuff."

"Okay then," said Waggit, "let's get going."

"I'd be happy for you to accompany me," she replied, "but I don't think it would be a good idea. You never know what a town is going to be like until you go there, and to be on the safe side I think it would be better if you stayed here."

He wasn't quite sure what she meant by this, but she seemed determined to leave without him. She saw this worried him, so she kneeled down and stroked his head.

"I will be away for a while, but I will return. In the

meantime stay close to the tent and don't worry. I'll be back in time for lunch."

Once again her soft voice and serene manner had a calming effect on him, and by the time she disappeared into the distance he was chewing contentedly on a stick. But as she left, so did the feeling of peace that surrounded her. The trees that had seemed soft, gentle, and protective a few minutes earlier now took on a more sinister quality, and he had the sensation of being trapped beneath them. He jumped at a sound behind him, only to see a white-tailed deer more nervous than he was running through the woods.

"I don't like it here," he muttered to the stick, having no one else to talk to. "I should have learned my lesson; I never should've let an Upright take over my life again. Tazar wouldn't. What if she's going to bring the Ruzelas back here? Maybe that's why she told me to stay by the tent so that I would be much easier to catch."

Miserable, lonely, and scared, he decided that it would be safer to move away from the camp. Between the edge of the woods and the bank of the river there were some tall rushlike grasses, and he hid in the middle of them. The hours passed slowly, because he did not dare to move. The sun wasn't strong, but after a while he still began to feel hot. The river was only a few feet away and he decided he would take a drink and cool off, so he left his hiding place and splashed about in the cold water. He began to feel more cheerful, and as his optimism returned, so did his independence.

Why, he thought, am I waiting for an Upright to bring me food? I can look after myself. There's no point hanging around waiting to see if she returns.

He decided to go hunting. He was a good hunter, fast, with a strong sense of smell, and smart enough to anticipate what moves his quarry would make next. But none of these qualities are of any use if there's no prey in the vicinity. He tracked back and forth through the woods, his nose working furiously, but the scent trails he picked up were all old. The animals that had left them were probably now resting in the cool of their burrows or out hunting for themselves in the surrounding fields. He saw a chipmunk scamper away, and a squirrel chattered at him in panic from the branch of a tree. Apart from these there was no sign of life.

There was nothing to do but go back to his hiding place, wait for Felicia to return, and hope that she was by herself. After what seemed like days he saw her lanky figure crossing the fields, several packages in her arms. He decided to stay hidden until he was certain that nobody else was with her. It was a good plan that turned out to be completely useless. Instead of going up to the tent, calling out his name, and then looking around for him, Felicia came directly to the edge of the rushes and said, "Waggit, why are you hiding in there? I'm so sorry to have left you, but as it turned out it was just as well you weren't with me."

How she knew he was there he had no idea, but it didn't matter because once again he felt calm and all fear left him. He didn't even feel awkward leaving his hiding place, by which time she was fussing around the opening of the tent.

"Oh, my goodness," she said, "those are the most unfriendly people I've met in a long time. They didn't want to sell me anything, even though I had the money. They finally condescended to overcharge me for a few necessary items, including . . ." She dug into the bottom of one of the brown paper sacks and pulled out a new, bright blue leash. "Ta-da. You're now respectable." And he let her clip it onto his collar, even though he wasn't crazy about it. "They didn't have a pet shop, of course, but I found it in the hardware store. However, even with your newfound respectability I think we will circumvent their hostility through circumnavigation."

Waggit frowned and cocked his head in confusion.

"We will avoid any possible confrontation by not going near that settlement again," she explained. "I did, however, stock up on food supplies."

This was good news for Waggit, who was feeling famished after his unsuccessful attempt at hunting.

"I got you some cans of real dog food," she said. "I think people at the store thought I was going to eat it myself."

For the life of him Waggit couldn't see why that would be considered strange. He had eaten human food from time to time, so why would humans eating dog food be any more unusual?

When they had both finished eating and Felicia had cleared away all the utensils, she sat down on the trunk of a fallen pine tree, broke off a long stalk of grass, and chewed it contemplatively. Waggit had noticed that this was a habit of hers whenever she was concentrating. She then unfolded a map that she had purchased that morning and studied it carefully.

"I really do think," she said after several minutes, "that it would be better if we bypass this town, and that we should do it at night. Unfortunately, whether we take the tracks or the roadway, they both go through its outskirts. We will just have to keep a very low profile and hope that nobody pays us any attention."

They left when it got dark. Although she had a flashlight in her backpack Felicia thought it was wiser not to use it while they were in open countryside, and so their progress was slow. When they got to the town they tried to keep to its edges, but because it was small avoiding the center was difficult. They rounded a corner, and there in front of them was a single story building with a big illuminated sign and brightly colored lights in the windows. Loud music came from inside, and parked in front were several cars and pickup trucks.

"Oh dear," said Felicia, "a bar. People in bars usually go one of two ways. They either get very jolly and silly or mean and belligerent. Let's see if we can find another way around it."

They turned back in the direction they came, and after a few blocks found a road that looked as if it would go around the edge of the town and still keep them on their route. They had gone just a short distance when Waggit suddenly stopped. His ears were pricked, and he turned his head back toward the bar. Over the sound of the music came the yelping of a dog that was obviously in pain and distress.

"Can you hear that?" Waggit asked.

"No," replied Felicia. "What is it?"

"There's a dog in trouble," said Waggit. "We have to go back."

6

The Rescue of the
Cowardly Pit Bull

Cautiously they crept along the side of the bar until they came to an alleyway that was at the rear of the building. Here they saw three men throwing rocks at a sturdy pit bull they had trapped between a wall and one of the bar's Dumpsters. The dog cowered in terror and yelped as each rock hit him. Already there were some places where he was cut and blood was starting to ooze. Felicia drew herself to her full height, which was considerable, and stepped into the alley.

"Let's stop that right now," she demanded in a

voice that was calm but authoritative.

The men looked around in surprise.

"Why don't you just move on and mind your own business?" one of them said.

"When innocent animals are being needlessly hurt, it *is* my business," replied Felicia. "It's everybody's business."

"Listen, you old hag, take that flea-bitten mutt of yours and get out of here now before we give you some of the same," yelled the man.

However, Felicia's calming influence seemed to be having some effect on the other two.

"We didn't mean to hurt it," said one of them, which was difficult to believe since he was holding a rock in both hands.

"We were scared of it," added the third, letting his rock drop to the ground as if trying to get rid of the evidence. "We thought it was going to attack us."

The sad creature huddled against the Dumpster didn't look as if it was able to attack a chipmunk, let alone three grown men.

"It's a pit bull," insisted the first man, who was clearly the leader, "and pit bulls are vicious—everyone knows that."

"No," said one of the others, "the lady's right. We shouldn't've been doing that. It weren't hurting us none."

"You see, ma'am," the third addressed Felicia, "we had a little too much to drink."

"You speak for yourself, Jimmy, you wimp," said the leader. "I'm stone-cold sober, and I don't want no pit bulls 'round this neighborhood, and no homeless people neither," he continued, looking at Felicia.

He picked up another rock and hurled it at the pit bull. The dog was frozen with terror and made no attempt to avoid being hit. It struck him hard on his back leg, and he let out another squeal of pain but still did not move. The rock thrower picked up another stone and prepared to aim it at the prostrate creature when Waggit suddenly ran toward him and delivered a sharp nip to the back of his ankle. Now it was the man's turn to howl, which he did as he hopped up and down on one foot while holding on to the other. Waggit took advantage of the man's unbalanced state by throwing his full weight at the back of his knee and bringing him crashing to the ground. Felicia, in the meantime, had taken hold of the pit bull by his collar and was dragging him away from the corner where he had been trapped.

The man was a good deal drunker than he had claimed and was finding it extremely difficult to get back on his feet. His friends had already fled, fearing that the commotion would attract unwanted attention. When the man finally managed to prop himself up on his arms, Waggit darted in and nipped his wrist, causing him to go down again. He lay on the pavement looking up at Felicia and the two dogs, hatred and anger burning in his eyes.

"I'll get you. I'll get all of you," he yelled. "I'm going to get my gun and my friends and don't think I won't."

"Boys," Felicia said to the two dogs, "we'd better get out of here as quickly as possible, because I think I believe him."

The three of them ran as fast as their legs would take them, which in Felicia's and Waggit's case was pretty fast. They took the darkest and quietest streets until they finally came out on the far side of the town. As they left the buildings behind they moved into rolling, open countryside, with narrow lanes and large fields surrounded by stone walls, inside which cows stood or lay. They could just make out a ridge of mountains silhouetted on the horizon. They paused to catch their breath. The pit bull was in some pain and was making sure everyone knew it.

"Ouch. Ow. I can't go on. It hurts."

As Felicia bent down to give the injuries a closer inspection, Waggit's ears pricked and his hackles went up.

"I can hear something coming this way," he warned.

Felicia stood to her full height and saw headlights in the distance.

"It's probably that awful man and some of his drunken pals," she said.

She looked around for somewhere to hide, but she could see none—no bushes or stands of trees or even any farm buildings that would afford them cover.

"Well," she said, looking at the herd of cows near-est them, "there's nothing to do but beg a favor from our cloven-hoofed friends."

Apart from the stone wall there was also a wire fence running around the perimeter of the field, and it pinged quietly, indicating that it was electri-fied. Despite Felicia's warnings, the pit bull managed to get zapped twice while scrambling through, even though Waggit made it with ease. When all three of them were in the field they approached the cows ten-tatively, Felicia leading the way. She went up to the nearest one, which chewed contemplatively. The animal had an unusually large set of horns for a female, and Waggit eyed them with concern.

"Good evening," Felicia began. "I wonder if you would do my two friends and me a favor. Some very bad men are pursuing us, and there are no hiding places in the vicinity. Would you and the other ladies mind if we sort of crouched down among you? We would be very quiet and still and cause no trouble, I assure you. Would that be okay?"

The cow looked at her with a baleful eye and said, "Moooooo."

"Oh dear," said Felicia, turning to the dogs. "I seem to have forgotten all my cow communication skills. One needs them so infrequently, and if you don't use them you certainly do lose them."

The cow still hadn't moved, so Waggit went as close to her as he dared, given the size of her horns, and growled in what he hoped was a menacing man-ner. It clearly wasn't very frightening because she just looked down at him disdainfully, but then slowly and unhurriedly she walked out of the way, allowing them access to the middle of the herd.

"Well, that works for me," said Felicia. "Come, boys, let's mingle quietly."

She got on all fours and crawled in between the cows. For a moment Waggit thought she might even start nibbling the grass as well, but she did not. He and the pit bull moved into the center also, although the latter seemed very jumpy, and not too happy with the arrangement. The three of them crouched down making sure that they each had a sleeping cow between them and the road. They had just gotten into this position when they heard the sound of a truck approaching. The dogs held their breath as the light from the headlights swept over the field, but the cows didn't move and the vehicle drove on without seeing them.

They remained in their positions for several minutes until it was obvious that their pursuers were not coming back. Then Felicia got up and turned to the herd.

"Thank you so much. Your help has been invaluable," she said.

The cows either didn't understand what she said or didn't care, for none of them paid her the slightest attention. Waggit looked around to see in which direction they should go. In the far corner of the field he could just see in the darkness the outline of some sort of building. The three of them hurried toward it. As they got closer they saw that it was a dilapidated, crude shelter, but still sufficient to provide them with some protection for the rest of the night.

The floor of the building was covered with old, damp hay that smelled sour, but which made it a little softer to lie on. Felicia took off her backpack and sat down on it. Waggit lay next to her, but the pit bull paced nervously back and forth at the hut's entrance.

"Relax," said Waggit, "they won't find us here."

"Yeah?" said the pit bull. "It's all very well for you to say 'Relax,' but you weren't the one they were throwing rocks at."

This was certainly true and seemed a valid point.

"What's your name?" Waggit asked, trying a different tactic to get the dog to calm down.

"Lug," replied the pit bull, clearly in no mood to engage in conversation.

"Mine's Waggit," said Waggit, "and this is Felicia."

"Very pleased to meet you, even under these

circumstances," Felicia said warmly. "Now I think we'd better take a look at what those dreadful men did to you." She went over to him and gently ran her hands over his body, inspecting the places where the rocks had done their damage. Then she got a first-aid kit from her backpack, squeezed some ointment out of a tube, and rubbed it into the places where the dog's skin had been broken. He made more fuss when she did this than when the men pelted him with the rocks that had made the wounds in the first place.

"Ow. Eeee. Be careful. Oooh, that stings" and other words to that effect came out in a constant stream of complaint.

"Goodness gracious," said Felicia, "what a fuss. Couldn't you be just a little more pit-bullish?"

"I'm very sensitive," whined Lug.

"You certainly are," agreed Felicia, "but if any of these get infected you'll be very sick as well."

Her first-aid work over, she decided that it was her bedtime. She took her sleeping bag off the backpack, unrolled it, removed her boots, and climbed in. Within minutes her gentle snoring indicated that she was fast asleep. The dogs, Lug in particular, were still too wired by the excitement of the evening's events to follow her.

"It did hurt when she put that stuff on," he said defensively.

Waggit made no comment.

"How come," Lug continued after a pause, "she can understand what we say, and we can understand her?"

"She just can," said Waggit. "She says all Uprights could if they tried, but they've forgotten how."

"Well, that's a blessing," declared Lug. "I wouldn't want them to know everything I said. That would be way too scary."

"I thought," said Waggit, "that pit bulls weren't scared of anything."

"That's the curse of our breed," Lug replied. "Everyone expects us to be fighters, and some of us just aren't. All I want is a quiet life, not this constant confrontation."

"Well," said Waggit, "I don't think your quiet life's going to start tonight, so you might as well get some sleep so you'll be ready for tomorrow."

"Sometimes it seems as if it's always going to be like this," Lug said with a mournful sigh, but he was to get no sympathy from the others, for Waggit was also drifting off to sleep. As he lost consciousness he could still hear the click of Lug's claws on the floor as he paced up and down.

7

Lug Tags Along

The following morning Felicia was already up when the dogs awoke. Waggit watched her sleepily as she dug into her backpack and pulled out some food for breakfast. This fascinated him because the bag always seemed to contain more stuff than it could possibly hold. He wasn't fascinated enough, however, to stop from eating the food she put in front of him—today's menu was cans of chipped beef and was lip-smackingly delicious.

When the meal was finished and Felicia had cleared

away the dishes, she stood up and looked around. What she saw wasn't encouraging; just field after field of rugged, rock-filled countryside mixed with thickly wooded areas that sometimes went on for miles. There were farm buildings in the distance, and already she could hear the sound of tractors and other equipment being started for the day's work. There were no major highways in view, nor any other form of transportation that would get them on their way. She turned to Lug.

"Are you from around here?" she inquired. "I'm not familiar with this area."

"I've lived here all my life," he answered.

"Tell me," she said, "how far are we from the railroad?"

"I don't know," replied Lug. "When I said I lived around here I meant in the town. I've never been this far out."

"It's over there," said Waggit, pointing his nose in one direction. "I can hear it; there's something going through now."

"You're right," agreed Lug. "I hear it now. It's slowing down. Oh, no, it's picking up speed again."

Felicia tilted her head to one side, straining to catch a sound.

"You dogs," she said. "Your hearing never ceases to amaze me. Well, that's the direction we should go." She turned toward Lug. "So," she said to him, "it's been a pleasure to meet you, and maybe our paths will cross again sometime. Try to keep those wounds as clean as possible, and you should be okay."

Lug appeared crestfallen, as if he was about to burst into tears.

"You mean . . . ?" His voice trembled. "You mean . . ."

"What's the matter?" asked Felicia.

"You mean," said Lug, "you're leaving me?"

"We have to," explained Felicia. "Waggit and I have a long journey to make. Besides, your family will be worried about you."

"I don't have a family," Lug said with a sigh.

"Nobody?" said Felicia. "You don't live with any people?"

"No," replied Lug. "The Upright at the bar feeds me from time to time, but he's the only one that I see a lot. Can't I come with you?"

Felicia considered this for a moment, but Waggit did not look happy with the suggestion.

"If Waggit doesn't mind, then I would have no

objection," she finally said.

"But he won't know anybody when he gets to New York," Waggit protested.

"I don't know anybody here," said Lug. "Or hardly anybody."

"But New York's a tough town," the other dog insisted.

"You mean they do worse there than throw rocks at you when they get drunk?" asked Lug fearfully.

"No, I suppose not," Waggit conceded. "I guess if Felicia doesn't mind, it's all right with me if you come with us."

"Thank you," said Lug. "You won't regret it."

Waggit was not so sure.

Felicia decided that they should try to complete at least part of the trip by train.

"Do they allow dogs on trains?" Waggit asked, not quite sure of what trains were.

"Bless you," said Felicia, "the trains we'll be traveling on don't even allow people on them. There hasn't been a passenger train in these parts for years. No, we'll be going freight."

Waggit wasn't quite sure what "going freight" meant either, but anything without people sounded good to him. They headed in the direction the noise of the train seemed to be coming from, wherever possible crossing fields and open countryside rather than roads. They stayed by the stone walls that marked the edges of the fields, trying to be inconspicuous. This also helped in one field, where a bull eyed them suspiciously. Felicia remembered the phrase in cattle language for "Good morning," which she yelled out to him cheerily, but it did nothing to improve his humor, and they were relieved to move on to the next meadow.

They had much better luck with four horses grazing in a paddock near one of the farms. At first they were as startled that Felicia could talk to them as both Waggit and Lug had been and, being horses, shied away nervously, but when they realized she was no threat they happily chatted with her for several minutes. They knew where the railroad was, and because they had covered the area extensively on trail rides, they were able to tell Felicia the best way to get there without attracting too much attention.

Finally the three travelers saw the embankment upon which the tracks ran, and they walked in the fields next to it with Felicia leading the way in complete silence. She was obviously looking for something.

"You said you heard the train slow down?" she asked the two dogs.

They replied that they had both heard it, but that it picked up speed again soon afterward.

"We need to find where it slowed," she explained, "because that will be the only place where we'll be able to get on board."

Waggit ran ahead, happy to have something to do. Every so often he would sprint up the bank, but he couldn't see anything that would cause the train to reduce speed. Suddenly the land went uphill until the tracks and the fields were on the same level. The rails went around a sharp bend, and then he saw it—a railroad crossing over a road with two barriers on either side, their arms pointing to the sky, followed by another steep turn in the track.

"Here," he yelled to the others. "This must be where the trains slow down."

Felicia and Lug hurried to catch up with him, Felicia striding along but Lug lumbering beside her, panting profusely.

"Well done, Waggit," she congratulated him. "You found it. This is the perfect place to wait."

She put her pack down on the grass next to the road

and sat on it, first of all taking out a bottle of water, some of which she drank, the rest of which she shared with the dogs. It was now around the middle of the day and the sun was quite hot. There was no shade, and the animals were soon panting. Several cars and trucks passed along the road, but their drivers paid no heed to the strangely dressed woman and the two dogs. Suddenly there was a clanging sound that made both dogs leap to their paws, and the barriers began to descend.

"Okay," said Felicia, "let's wait until we see a suitable car, one that we can jump on to."

"I can't jump," whined Lug, "at least not very well."

"This comes as no surprise," she remarked, looking at his chunky body, "so I will help you get on board before I jump myself. Waggit will go first since he's the fastest."

"If he's the fastest, why doesn't he go last?" complained Lug.

Waggit was beginning to find the dog's constant grumbling a little irritating, but he tried to answer him as patiently as he could.

"You see, if I'm already on the train I can help

Felicia get you on board quicker. That will give her more time to get on herself."

"Absolutely correct, Waggit," Felicia declared. "Now let's get ready."

The sound of the approaching train was getting louder, and as it came into sight it blew two sharp blasts of its whistle.

"Look for a car that has enough space for the three of us to sit comfortably," said Felicia while she secured the pack to her back.

As it came closer to the crossing the train slowed to almost walking pace. The engine groaned as it went by, straining to pull its long line of wagons. The first of these had a large cylindrical tank mounted on it that left no room for anyone, either dog or human, to sit. They waited tensely as car after car passed, each one identical to the first.

"Oh, come on," said Felicia. "There must be something else on a train as long as this."

But as it turned out there wasn't. After what seemed like hours the last tanker car passed, pushed by another engine at the rear.

"What rotten luck," said Felicia. "Now we'll have to wait for the next one."

"Why don't we walk on a little way while we're waiting?" Waggit asked, longing to get out of the sun.

"I don't think that's a good idea," said Felicia. "We'll never get a spot better than this. It's worth waiting here. The train has to slow for both the crossing and the bend, and when the locomotive goes around the curve the engineer can't see us get on, so it's perfect. I know it's hot, but with a bit of luck we won't have to wait too long."

Luck, however, seemed to be in short supply that day, and it was hours before the dogs' ears pricked up at the sound of the next train. By that time they were dispirited and irritable, and even Felicia's soothing influence was beginning to wear thin. Waggit actually growled at Lug when the pit bull lay down too close to him. Their mood wasn't improved any by the fact that once again the first cars on this train were tankers, but then they saw a line of boxcars that looked promising. As they rumbled past, Felicia stood back a little bit so that she could get a better look at what was coming.

"That one," she said, pointing to a car, the doors of which were open. "That is the best."

This train was moving faster than the previous one, but Waggit was easily able to leap aboard. He turned to look and see how the other two were doing. Lug was lumbering along, more or less keeping up, with Felicia close behind him, although she was slowed down by the weight and size of her backpack. She bent down and grabbed the pit bull by the scruff of his neck and threw him into the car. Then her foot caught in one of the railroad ties, and with a cry of pain she fell beside the track.

8

Freight Train to Nowhere

Waggit looked out of the doors to see Felicia on the ground, rolling over and over.

"Felicia," he yelled in panic, but she did not reply. He didn't know what to do next. If he leapt out to help her, Lug would be left by himself in the boxcar, unable to get out, and if he didn't he would be separated from her maybe forever. All day long he had been regretting his agreement to let the pit bull join them but no time more so than now.

The decision to jump or not was nearly made for

him as the train lurched forward and almost pitched him back onto the tracks, but he managed to regain his balance and stay on his paws. The train was beginning to pick up speed, and when he looked out again Felicia was nowhere to be seen.

"This is terrible," Lug said.

"It is," agreed Waggit.

"We'll never get to New York now," continued the pit bull. "I mean, she's the only one who knows the way. Who's going to look after us if she's not here?"

"Actually," said Waggit irritably, "I was thinking more along the lines of wouldn't it be terrible if she's hurt herself."

"You're absolutely right," said Lug. "If she's hurt herself she'll never be able to catch up with us, plus she's got all the food."

Waggit was beginning to realize that it was useless to talk to Lug about anything that didn't directly affect him, and sympathy for the plight of another simply wasn't something he felt. So he said nothing, sat down, and looked around. The car had obviously been used to transport animals of some kind, and it still smelled of them and their hay.

Lug was adding his own smell of fear, and despite

himself Waggit felt sorry for him. He seemed scared of everything and everyone, and here he was stuck in a train car that he couldn't get out of that was going who knew where with a dog he'd met just the day before. The only reason he had wanted to come with them in the first place was that he was more frightened of going back to the town than he was of the journey.

"It'll be okay," Waggit assured him, sounding more confident than he felt.

"I dunno," said Lug. "I hope you're right."

"How come if you never lived with Uprights you've got a name?" Waggit asked, trying to take the other dog's mind off his present situation by changing the subject.

"The Upright at the bar," replied Lug, "the one that used to feed me. He started to call me big lug, and it just sort of stuck. How about you? You've got a strange name. How did you get yours?"

"The team gave it to me," said Waggit. "When I was younger my tail used to wag a lot when I was excited or scared and so that's why they called me Waggit."

"What's the team?" asked Lug.

"Oh, they're a pack of dogs that I lived with in the park. They saved my life. I'm going back to them when

I get to New York, if they'll have me, if there still is a team, of course."

"Can I join the team when we get there?" Lug asked. "If we get there."

"Let's see *when* we get there," said Waggit, emphasizing the *when* to reassure himself as much as Lug.

The two dogs became silent and morosely looked out the open doors as the countryside sped by. It was beginning to get dark now, and the darker it got the worse their fears became. Objects that they would have hardly noticed during the day flashed past like great, threatening black masses. The two of them edged farther and farther away from the open doors until, without realizing it, they were both in the far corner of the car, huddled together for comfort. Then, as fatigue overcame them and they were rocked by the "clackety-clack" rhythm of the train, they finally fell asleep.

Sometime later they were awoken by the screeching sound of metal on metal as the train slowed down and changed direction. When it had settled into its new course it didn't pick up speed, however, but proceeded at a slow pace, and then gradually came to a stop with much hissing of brakes and clanging of steel.

It was still dark, and the two dogs were scared of what might happen next. An eerie silence surrounded them, and Waggit summoned all his courage and peered out, but he could only see blackness.

"What do we do now?" asked Lug, his voice quavering with fear.

"I don't know," said Waggit. "I don't know whether we should stay here or jump down and run."

"Jump?" cried Lug incredulously. "Jump? I can't jump. It's too high. I'd break every bone in my body."

"Better that than be caught by the Ruzelas and get taken to the Great Unknown," Waggit assured him. "I know—I've been there and I'd take broken bones and freedom any day."

"What's a Ruzela?" asked Lug.

"They're people that all wear the same stuff and try to catch you," said Waggit.

"What's the Great Unknown?" asked Lug.

"It's where they take dogs that have been caught. I was caught once," said Waggit.

"If you've been there and know what it's like, why is it called the Great Unknown?" inquired Lug.

"Because I'm the only one who ever made it back alive," replied Waggit.

"So why if——" began Lug.

Waggit cut him short.

"Will you stop asking questions?" he said irritably. "They're not going to help us get out of here. Be quiet while I think."

Lug fell sulkily silent while Waggit assessed the situation. The train might start again in a few minutes, but as he looked out the open door he thought this was unlikely. They had stopped in an area full of boxcars similar to the one they were in, and many of them looked as if they had been there for some time. Weeds had begun to grow around the tracks and underneath some of the cars. If the two dogs remained there and a railroad worker came along and closed the door, they would be trapped. Waggit decided what they should do.

"Lug," he said, "come and stand by the door and keep watch. There's something I have to do."

Without questioning what it was, Lug went to the opening and cautiously peered out. As he did Waggit ran up and, with his shoulders against the other's rear end, pushed him with all his might, and the two of them tumbled out of the car and onto the tracks.

"Ow, ow," complained Lug. "What did you do that

for? I'm already injured as it is. Didn't you think about that?"

"We had to get out of there or risk being caught inside, and I knew you wouldn't jump by yourself," he replied. "We're better off out here. I don't think this train's going anywhere. The rest of the journey's going to be on paw."

Before Lug could complain again they both heard the sound of footsteps walking along the tracks in the distance.

"Quick," said Waggit, "under here."

They both dived under the wheels of a boxcar that was surrounded by weeds. It was a good hiding place, except that some seeds from a dandelion got caught on Lug's nose and caused him to let out a thunderous sneeze. The sound of the footsteps stopped and the two dogs froze.

"Waggit. Lug. Is that you? Where are you?"

Waggit peered out excitedly from between the wheels.

"It's Felicia," he barked with joy, and ran over to where she was standing.

"Oh, it *is* you. I'm so glad to see you both," she said, stroking their heads, "but we've got to get out of here. And you've got to be quiet."

"Felicia, are you all right?" asked Waggit in a low voice.

"I'm fine," she replied, "a bit bruised but otherwise unharmed."

"But how did you get here?" Waggit asked.

"Well," Felicia said, "after I fell I picked myself up, and as luck would have it another car like this was passing. I just managed to scramble on board before it was going too fast." She looked at Lug. "You, young man, are very heavy. I didn't realize until I picked you up, and it was because of that I lost my balance."

"It's not my fault," whined Lug. "It was the bar. They ate very fatty food at the bar."

"It doesn't matter," said Felicia. "What does matter is that we're all back together again. Now we've got to get out of here before it gets light."

Suddenly in the distance Waggit heard the crunch of boots on gravel. Once again they had to dive under the boxcar, only this time Lug's nose was fortunately itch-free. Then they saw the beam of a flashlight, and the crunching sound got closer. They held their breath. The workman carrying the light came up to the car they had been in, and the yellow beam washed its interior. Then they heard the sound that Waggit had feared, and the reason he had wanted to get out—the rumbling noise of the door being closed and the snap of the bolt as it was pushed into the locked position. The man moved from car to car, and the sound of his boots got softer as he went farther down the long train until it could no longer be heard. After that close call even Lug needed no more persuading that getting out of there was a really good idea.

In the pitch black the three of them stumbled through the rail yard as best they could. They had to climb over several tracks before they could get to flat ground. Even when they accomplished this the going was still difficult because the night was so dark. A tall chain-link fence ran alongside the outermost tracks, and garbage had collected between it and the rails. Waggit found himself stumbling over empty beer bottles, soda cans, bits of old clothing, and paper bags that still retained the tantalizing smell of hamburgers. At one point Lug got caught up in some electrical cable, which Felicia had to disentangle. It was not pleasant, but at least they were leaving the man with the flashlight behind. Then, as dawn broke, it became much easier, not only because they could see better, but also because they were now farther away from the railroad tracks.

The fence suddenly ended for no apparent reason, and they were able to head away from the tracks. After crossing some fields they came to a narrow road. Felicia clipped Waggit's leash to his collar and tied a length of baling twine that she had found on the train around Lug's neck. It was still early and the road they were on wasn't one that was ever busy, so the three of them walked along unconcerned with the possibility of passing traffic. It was good to be in open country again, and they all were in a lighthearted mood. Lug even forgot to complain about his injuries anymore, and Felicia whistled in a tuneless but contented way. They had been walking for about an hour when she suddenly stopped on the brow of a small hill. In front of them in the distance they could see a wide highway snaking down the valley.

"I think I know this area," she said. "If I'm not mistaken there's a diner near here called Truckers. If we could find it that would be a really good thing, because there may be some friends there who could help us."

She looked around, peering hard, trying to see where it was.

"I'm pretty certain it's around here somewhere, but where exactly?"

The two dogs looked at each other, put their noses in the air, and slowly turned their heads. Suddenly Waggit closed his eyes, took a deep breath, and smiled.

"Ah, hamburgers," he said.

Lug's head was pointing in the same direction and he also had the same look of bliss on his face.

"Mmm, French fries," he said with a sigh.

To one side of the paved road that they were standing on was a farm road, no more than a rough track, really, but it was going in the same direction the smells were coming from. Waggit pulled toward it, stopped, and turned to Felicia and Lug.

"This'll take us there," he said. "Come on, follow me."

9

Truckers and the Big Rigs

The road was deeply rutted from the tractors that had driven on it when it was muddy. Their wheels had also churned up large rocks and stones that added to the difficulties Felicia and the two dogs encountered as they made their slow progress along it.

"This may be heading in the right direction," she said. "But that's the only thing it's got going for it. Let's sit for a while. I've got to rest."

She took off her backpack and sat on it. The dogs

settled down next to her, secretly glad that she needed a break.

"Who are these friends you were talking about, the ones who might be able to help us?" asked Waggit. "And where are they?"

"Not too far from here, I hope," was her reply.

"Hope?" said Lug, alarmed.

"Well, you see, the problem is they drive big rigs," she continued, "and you're never quite sure where they will be, but they all stop at Truckers if they're in the area. There's one in particular that I hope will be there."

"How do you know them?" asked Waggit.

"Oh, from being around," she replied enigmatically.

"From being around what?" demanded Lug, who liked details.

"Let's just say that we have a lot in common, the drivers and me," said Felicia. "We're all roamers at heart. They do it for a trucking company, and I do it for myself."

After Felicia had gathered up her things they set off once again down the rock-strewn track. Waggit's paws were sore and his legs ached, and he wanted to be on his way to the park, not scrambling down some country road. He realized that he was longing to get back to the team and to familiar surroundings. He worried about whether they would have him back. After all, he had left them to live with a human, and he knew that Tazar considered this to be disloyalty verging on treachery. But they had always been a generous, warm, and forgiving group of animals, and furthermore he had been the team's best hunter. As for Lug, well, Waggit would worry about him when they got there.

The track had been cut through one of the many woods in the area. As they came through the trees they heard the hum of traffic, and then they saw a highway winding through the valley.

"Not too far from here," said Felicia cheerfully, "and the food is pretty good. You'll both like it anyway. They serve the best meatloaf in the county."

In the distance Waggit caught sight of a building made out of shiny metal that gleamed silver in the sunlight, with a huge electric sign flashing in front of it. It was surrounded by an enormous parking lot full of the biggest trucks he had ever seen.

"There it is," said Felicia fondly. "Good old Truckers."

As they got closer the trucks seemed to get bigger, the building shinier, and the lights flashier. Great snorting vehicles came and went, with the occasional car weaving between them to avoid getting squashed. Men and women bustled in or out of the restaurant; everyone seemed to be in a hurry. To Waggit it was exciting, almost like being in his beloved city. Recent events had taught Lug, however, to be wary of buildings with lights, noise, and many people, and he pulled back on his twine leash.

"It's okay," said Felicia. "These are my friends. They won't hurt you. I won't let them."

As she said this she bent down and stroked him the length of his spine. He stopped pulling and trotted along by her side. They were walking up to the diner when a large truck pulled in front of them and stopped. The window slid down and a cheery face poked out.

"Hey there, duchess," said the man to whom it belonged. "I haven't seen you in a dog's age. And talking of dogs, when did you get that mangy pair? I don't like the look of that one." He nodded at Lug. "He looks mean. Still, I suppose a woman needs a dog like that for protection."

"Well," Felicia replied with a smile, "if he scares a

tough guy like you then I guess he's doing his job."

"I didn't say I was scared of him," said the man. "I just said he looks mean. By the way, your friend's parked over there. I think he's taking a nap."

"Which direction's he heading?" asked Felicia.

"South, I believe," said the man, "but you'd better ask him. I gotta be going, time's a-wasting. I'll see you around."

The window of the huge truck whirred as it closed. There was a deafening noise as the gears engaged and the vehicle slowly rumbled off. Felicia waved and then led the two animals across the parking lot. She looked around at all the parked vehicles until she saw one that she walked toward. It had a bright yellow cab, and on the side were painted the words *Yellow Wood Trucking, Lawrence, Massachusetts, Archibald Frost, Owner*.

There was a metal step at the side of the cab, and Felicia used this to raise herself up and bang sharply on the window.

"Frosty, it's Felicia," she shouted. "Open up."

From deep inside the cab a voice was heard to say, "Go away! Can't a guy get any sleep around here?"

"You must be getting old, Frosty," said Felicia. "You never used to sleep at all."

There was the sound of movement in the cab, and then a face peered drowsily through the window. It was a man's face, and it was surrounded by an enormous white beard that would have made him look like Santa Claus were it not for the fact that the hair covering his top lip and running down the sides of his mouth was jet black. This made him look rather like a skunk. The other prominent feature of his face was the deep creases at the edges of each eye that indicated the man like to laugh a lot.

"Felicia," he said, "why didn't you say it was you?"

"I did," answered Felicia, "at the top of my lungs. You're not only getting old, you're getting deaf."

"Well, thank you, Felicia. It's nice to see you, too." He smiled.

"I'm only teasing," said Felicia. "You know I have a warm spot in my heart for you. Come on down. I want to introduce you to two friends."

When the door opened after a couple of minutes, the rest of Archibald Frost could be seen, and a very large rest it was too. He had an enormous stomach that pulled the front of his denim bib overalls tight. Beneath them he wore a red shirt with the sleeves rolled up to reveal two muscular arms and huge hands. Despite his size he moved delicately as he jumped to the ground.

"These are your friends?" he asked without a trace of surprise. "What are their names?"

"This one's Waggit," replied Felicia, "and this is Lug."

"I'm very pleased to meet you boys," said Frosty, "and how did you hook up with this disreputable woman?"

"Our paths crossed," Felicia answered for them, "and we decided to travel together."

"And what's the destination that will mark the end of this journey?" asked Frosty.

"Central Park," said Felicia.

"And I suppose you want me to take the three of you there?" He smiled, as if he knew this was exactly what she wanted.

"You know what I like about you, Frosty?" said Felicia. "You get straight to the point with no messing around, and you don't ask why a woman and two dogs in the middle of nowhere would want to go to Central Park."

"Well," he remarked, "I have enough trouble making my own decisions without questioning yours."

"The answer, of course, is yes, we would love to

have you drive us there. Is that a possibility?"

"It might be if you bought me lunch," said Frosty.

"Deal," said Felicia.

So Frosty locked the door of his truck and the four of them headed toward the silver diner.

10

Hitching a Ride

After a lengthy argument with the waitress in the diner Felicia finally conceded that the dogs would not be allowed inside. Instead she tethered them both to the handle of a newspaper vending machine. It wasn't something she liked to do, but leaving them loose would not only attract attention, it would be danger-ous with the big rigs that were constantly moving in and out of the parking lot. The only other alternative would have been to lock them in the cab of the truck, and she preferred to keep them where they could see her. The only flaw in the arrangement was that when a customer purchased a paper the dogs were pulled forward a few inches. Fortunately newspaper reading wasn't very popular with the diner's clients, especially when they had to negotiate a pit bull to get one, and so it turned out to be not too much of a problem.

Lug was very worried about being left outside.

"She will come back, won't she?" he asked Waggit.

"Of course she will," he replied. "Look, you can see her through the window. There's no way she could leave without us knowing it."

Waggit realized that he was reassuring himself as much as Lug, but the other dog's fears made him feel braver. When a dog in the cab of a passing truck barked at them furiously, Lug leapt back and nearly pulled the vending machine over.

"Don't worry about him," Waggit comforted Lug. "He's in the truck and can't get to us. And if he could I'd protect you."

All their fears were soothed when a waitress came out with two plates of meatloaf, placed one in front of each dog, scratched them behind the ears, and left. Whether or not it was the best meatloaf in the county, as Felicia had claimed, was a matter of opinion; that it was the fastest consumed in the county was indisputable. When Felicia and Frosty finally emerged she released the two dogs from the machine and the four of them walked back to the truck.

As Frosty opened the door to the cab he turned to Felicia and said, "Now, you know that I'm not allowed to take riders because of the insurance, so you'll all have to stay out of sight in the sleeper."

"Whatever you say, Frosty," said Felicia. "We're in your debt and will go wherever you want."

Frosty muttered something about debt having nothing to do with it and climbed up into the cab. Felicia passed him up her backpack.

"Goodness gracious, woman," he said as he labored to lift it up, "what have you got in here?"

"My entire life," said Felicia.

"Well, you have a very full life is all I can say," said Frosty.

"Indeed I do, and it seems," she said as she lifted Waggit up, "to be getting fuller by the day."

Frosty grabbed hold of Waggit by the loose skin at the back of his neck, which, if done properly as the man did, doesn't hurt a dog. He lifted him over the two front seats and gently lowered him behind them. Waggit looked around and was amazed by what he saw. The back of the cab was like a small room, almost fully taken up by a neatly made bed with lots of frilly satin cushions on it that didn't look like the kind of thing Frosty would like at all. The roof of the compartment was quilted, and on either side there were some small storage cupboards. On top of one was a television, and on the other a framed photograph of a jolly, plump woman with her arms folded and a broad smile on her face.

It all felt cozy and safe to Waggit, and he jumped up onto the bed, turned around a couple of times, and settled down. His satisfaction with the situation was interrupted by Lug's yelping as Frosty repeated the process on him. Although Waggit was pretty certain that the dog wasn't being hurt, despite his wounds, it sounded as if Frosty was torturing him. This was followed by some groaning from Felicia as she hauled herself up, but finally the door was shut and they were ready to roll.

"It's going to be a long trip," Frosty warned. "I've got a heavy load, and with all these hills we aren't going to be moving fast."

"That's good," said Felicia diplomatically, "because that means I'll have the pleasure of your company for even longer."

Frosty turned toward her from his seat and grinned.

"Even if it means we'll be divided by a curtain?" he said as he pulled across the gray, pleated drape that divided the sleeping compartment from the driver's area.

"Even then," said Felicia, taking off her boots and nestling into the pillows, pulling the two dogs closer to her.

Waggit was surprised at how quiet the sound of the motor was from inside the truck. The vehicle was relatively new and the ride was smooth. He felt comfortable and safe with Felicia's arm around him, and best of all they were heading in the right direction—toward the park. This was better than the train in every respect.

"Frosty says that he won't be able to take us all the way," Felicia warned the dogs. "He has a tight deadline, but he'll get us as close as he can. We'll have to manage the last part by ourselves."

Frosty, of course, was unaware of the exchanges

between Felicia and the dogs, and anyway was too busy maneuvering the truck through the traffic to pay much attention to anything else. Like the rest of their kind, Waggit and Lug tended to sleep when there was nothing more interesting happening, and since there seemed to be very little else to do in a sleeper cab, they decided to let it live up to its name. Felicia read as they napped and had occasional conversations with Frosty as he drove, although, being a good driver, he kept these brief so that he could concentrate on guiding the big rig.

It was his policy to stop every two or three hours. After one such rest he didn't close the curtain completely, leaving a gap that Waggit could look through as he sat on the bed. It was dark now, and the truck's dashboard glittered with colored lights. The dog watched the red taillights of the other vehicles going in the same direction as them, and blinked against the glare of the headlights of the cars headed the other way. He felt sorry for them, leaving the city, and wondered if they knew what lay ahead of them. He was pretty sure they would soon come back if they knew what was good for them.

Frosty saw him looking at the traffic.

"Come up here," he said. "Nothing in my insurance says I can't have a dog in the cab. Come on."

He waved his arm indicating that Waggit should sit in the passenger seat. Cautiously the dog moved forward, not quite sure whether or not this was what Frosty wanted him to do.

"Come on, young man, hop up," said Frosty, giving him a helping hand.

When Waggit finally settled into the seat he was thrilled at the view that he got, and also the feeling of being special. Here he was doing something that apparently even Felicia wasn't allowed to do. He watched Frosty steer the truck on the highway with his strong muscular arms and huge hands, his eyes constantly checking the mirrors for other traffic. Waggit felt safe, and this sensation made him drowsy, so he turned around a couple of times in the big seat, lay down, and soon was fast asleep.

He was awoken by the sensation of the truck slowing down, and when he opened his eyes he saw that they were pulling into a gas station. When they were finally at a dead stop Frosty turned around and opened the curtain to reveal that Felicia and Lug had also been dozing. How much time had passed Waggit had no idea, but now there was little traffic on the road.

"Felicia," said Frosty, "time to wake up."

Felicia yawned and stretched, rubbed her eyes, and looked around.

"Where are we?" she asked.

"This is where I have to drop you off," he replied. "I'm sorry I can't take you any farther, but if I don't get this load to Port Newark on time they'll have my hide. You're only about ten or fifteen miles from midtown here."

"Is it late?" she asked. She, too, had noticed the lack of traffic.

"It's about three in the morning," Frosty said, "but this is a safe area. You'll be all right—besides, you've got the dogs to protect you."

She looked at the sleepy animals and smiled.

"Fond as I am of these two," she said to Frosty, "I wouldn't rely on them to keep me from harm. But you're right, we'll be okay, and I thank you for the lift. You're a good, kind man."

Frosty shrugged uncomfortably and almost blushed.

"It's no more than any friend would do," he mumbled.

Then he opened the door and helped them out. After he and Felicia hugged each other the big man got back into the cab and edged the truck onto the highway, gathering speed until his taillights vanished from view.

Waggit looked around. The gas station was in a commercial area with other businesses that were now closed. There was a road that went under the highway, and on the far side he could see neat, well-kept suburban houses.

"That's the direction I think we should go, don't you?" asked Felicia as she put on her backpack and gathered up the two dogs' leashes. They each sniffed the air a couple of times and approved her decision. The three of them set off, passing house after house, all of them very similar, with small front yards and one car parked in the driveway. It was very quiet, and not a soul was around. The only sound they heard was the occasional barking from dogs warning them to stay away from their turf. Waggit realized that if it wasn't for Felicia he would be scared, and even with her he was a little nervous.

"I've never liked the suburbs," she said, as if she was feeling the same way. "They seem to be neither one thing or another."

Using her flashlight she studied her map, turning it this way and that, and scratched her head.

"I can't make head nor tail out of where we are from this," she said, turning to Waggit. "What does your nose say?"

Waggit turned around, but there was no tingling sensation at all.

"I think my nose is lost too," he said.

"We're all tired," said Felicia. "Let's find somewhere to sleep, and in the morning maybe our noses and maps will make more sense."

Finding somewhere to sleep was easier said than done, however. They kept on walking, but all the streets looked alike. They seemed to be getting nowhere. Then they saw the glow of some streetlights in the distance and headed in that direction. After a few wrong turns down dead ends they came upon what looked like a village center. There were stores and a church, and an official-looking building that could be a town hall. Next to this was a park. It had black iron railings all around it, but the gates were open, and although it was small it was well kept, with a fountain in the center surrounded by flowerbeds and trees and shrubs along the edges.

"What's this?" Waggit asked Felicia.

"It's a park," she answered.

"It's not the park!" said Waggit with a derisory growl.

"I didn't say it was *the* park," said Felicia. "I said it was *a* park. It's also probably the best place to get some sleep."

She led the two dogs inside the gates and looked around. At the far end there was a chain-link fence. The bushes and shrubs in front of it were overgrown, as if the gardeners had run out of energy before they got to them. Felicia saw that there was a space between some of the bushes and the fence that would be just big enough to pitch the tent. She proceeded to do this, and in no time they were zipping up the front opening with the three of them safely inside. As the warmth from their bodies heated its interior they all fell deeply asleep. As it turned out their sleep was to be brief. It was no more than half an hour after they had settled down when the tent was lit up by a powerful beam of light and a loud voice said:

"People in the tent, this is the police. Come out with your hands up."

11

Trapped by Fear

Inside the tent its occupants sprang awake. Waggit's
tail wagged ferociously, a sure sign that he was
scared.

"Who's outside, and what did he say?" he whispered
to Felicia.

"It's a policeman," she replied, "and he told us to
put up our hands."

"We don't have hands," whined Lug. "What are we
going to do?"

"I'd better handle this," said Felicia. "It's a human-to-human situation. Just stay calm and don't growl."

She unzipped the opening of the tent and stuck her hands through it.

"I'm coming out," she shouted, and crawled out on her hands and knees. The dogs followed, tails down and ears flat to their heads. They were confronted by a rather elderly and overweight officer holding his gun and flashlight together in both hands. He was obviously as nervous as they were, because both the weapon and the lamp shook considerably, causing the beam of light to wobble back and forth.

"Keep your hands where I can see 'em," he said.

Felicia did as she was told and stood up with her hands over her head. She was a good six inches taller than the policeman, and with her arms raised she towered over him.

"Do you have any weapons?" he asked.

"Goodness gracious, no," said Felicia, "unless of course you count my Swiss Army knife, but that's in my backpack in the tent."

"Ma'am, what are you doing in a tent in the park?" he asked. He seemed confused by her, as if she wasn't what he was expecting.

"My dogs and I were sleeping," Felicia explained.

"But it's a park," he said. "You can't pitch a tent in the park."

"Actually," said Felicia, trying to sound as reasonable as she could, "it's the only place around here that you can."

"That's not the point," said the policeman. "You're not supposed to camp in this area at all. It's the suburbs, not Yellowstone."

"Well," said Felicia, "we had to sleep somewhere, didn't we? Now can we stop this silliness and let me put my hands down? I'm clearly not a threat."

She dropped her arms without waiting for permission. The policeman, sensing that he was getting nowhere in this discussion, changed tactics. He looked at the dogs.

"Do you have licenses for those two?" he asked.

"We're from way upstate," said Felicia. "You don't need licenses where we come from."

"Well," said the officer, "you're not upstate now, and around here dogs need to be licensed. If yours aren't, I'm going to have to call the Animal Control officer and have her take them into custody until you complete the necessary paperwork."

Although Waggit couldn't understand the

conversation between the two of them, he was becoming increasingly panicked. He still had a deep fear of Ruzelas. Just seeing this man brought back terrible memories of being captured by park rangers and taken to the pound. He remembered the nightmarish ride in the dog catcher's truck to the Great Unknown, and being put in a cage. The policeman asked Felicia for ID, and she dropped the leashes in order to get her wallet out of her back pocket. It was at that moment that Waggit made his decision.

He edged around so that he was behind Felicia. From this position there was nobody between him and the gate. As Felicia and the policeman were discussing her ID, he ran as fast as his legs would take him. Unfortunately so did Lug, whose ability to move quickly was nothing compared to Waggit's. Waggit realized that the lumbering dog was following him, and he stopped, wondering what to do.

He could hear Felicia shout, "Boys, come back! Please come back!"

I can't, he thought. I've got to get away.

Then he looked at Lug, panting and wheezing, his large body rolling as he moved, and he just couldn't abandon him there, so he ran back and took the leash that Lug was dragging behind him in his mouth and pulled the dog as fast as they both could go. They ran like this for several blocks until Lug gasped, "Waggit, you've got to stop. I can't go on."

It was clear that the overweight animal was exhausted, and so Waggit looked around for somewhere to hide. The street they were on had a house where renovations were being made, and in front of it was a large green Dumpster. Leaning against it was a plank of wood that the workers used for their wheelbarrows. They would run them up the plank, tip the contents out into the container, and then bring them down the same way. Waggit dragged the protesting Lug up it. When he got to the top he peered over. Even in the darkness he could see that it was only about one third full, and the drop from the plank to the bottom was considerable. Just then he heard the sound of a motor and saw the headlights of a vehicle coming their way. Another wave of terror overtook him, and with Lug's leash in his mouth, he leapt into the darkness of the Dumpster.

The two of them crashed on top of each other, rolling over and over. Fortunately the last thing that the workers had thrown into the container was some old insulation material, so their landing was soft but itchy. Little bits of fiberglass stuck to their coats, causing Waggit to scratch ferociously. It was worse for Lug, whose wounds were still not fully healed.

"What did you do that for?" he panted, still out of breath. "We could've landed on anything, broken glass even."

This was true, and Waggit felt ashamed that his fear might have caused them both harm.

"Well," he said defensively, "at least we're safe in here for the moment."

"Oh, we're safe all right," said Lug, "so safe that we may never be able to get out until they dump more stuff in here. Unfortunately, of course, that will be on top of us."

Waggit looked up at the rim of the Dumpster and realized that Lug, who was an expert on such matters, was right. There was no way they would ever be able to climb out. What had appeared to be a safe hiding place was now a prison. He cursed himself for giving in to panic. For the second time in as many days he was stuck with the pit bull, not knowing what to do next.

"What should we do?" Lug asked.

"I don't know," Waggit replied. "I don't know."

The two dogs fell silent, Waggit trying to work out a solution to their problem and Lug wandering around sniffing at things. After a few moments Lug started to dig in one corner.

"Well," he said, triumphantly, "it's not *all* bad news."

In his mouth he was holding the remains of a barbecued chicken that had been lunch for one of the workers. Waggit was so angry with himself that he couldn't eat any of it, which didn't seem to upset Lug at all. To the sound of bones being crunched, Waggit turned ideas over in his head, rejecting one after the other until he suddenly sat up.

"I know what might work," he said.

"What?" mumbled Lug through a mouthful of food.

"You know how sometimes Felicia seems to know what you're thinking and even where you are?" asked Waggit. He remembered the time when she came right up to the tall grass by the river and knew exactly where he was hiding.

"Can't say I do," replied Lug, "but you know her better than me."

"Well, she does," said Waggit. "So why don't we both close our eyes and concentrate on her and maybe she'll pick up our thoughts. Maybe she'll hear us thinking."

"Suit yourself," said Lug. "It seems nuts to me, but we've got nothing better to do."

Waggit was annoyed that Lug seemed to be criticizing his plan, since all he had contributed to the solution was a couple of belches, but he let it go. If his idea had a chance of succeeding he would have to have a clear and open mind. So the two dogs closed their eyes and tried to think as hard as they could about Felicia. At least Waggit did. Lug tried, but after a couple of minutes he fell asleep, the chicken having calmed his fears for the moment.

Waggit continued to concentrate, putting everything else out of his mind. Suddenly he heard Felicia's voice in his head, but it was broken up, like a bad cell phone connection.

"Waggit . . . me, Felicia . . . tell . . . louder . . . think . . ."

He tried as hard as he could to think louder, which is very difficult to do. Then he heard her voice in his head again.

"Waggit, are you getting me now? Where are you?"

"We're trapped in a Dumpster about six or seven blocks from the park."

"Well . . . I . . . the thing . . . quite useless."

Then she was gone, and there was nothing in his head.

Waggit lay in the Dumpster listening to the world come to life. It was quite light now, and car doors were slammed and engines started as their owners went off to work. School buses and trucks rumbled by, and occasionally there was the shrill whine of a motorbike speeding past. The longer they lay there the more Waggit despaired of Felicia ever finding them. He put his head on his paws and sighed often.

Then he heard footsteps coming up to the Dumpster. Could it be her? He tried thinking really hard to make sure she didn't walk by. No, the boots were coming toward them. Then a head peered over the top of the container, but it wasn't her. It was a man with a big mustache and a red handkerchief tied around his head.

"What the . . .?" he cried as he saw the two animals. "Hey, Charlie, come and see what we've got here."

In a few moments another face appeared, that of another man.

"Well, well," the second man remarked. "And what are you two doing in there? Came looking for food, I've no doubt, and then couldn't get out. Come on, Ron, let's give them a hand."

"Are you kidding?" said the first man. "And get bitten to death? I don't like the look of that one"—he pointed to Lug—"and the other's big enough that I'm not going to take him on."

"I suppose you're right," agreed the second man. "No point in taking risks, although they're not strays. They've got leashes on."

"Just because that nasty-looking one's got a bit of string around his neck doesn't mean he's not a stray or that he doesn't have rabies," said the other. "I think we should call the cops. They'll get them out of there."

He took out his cell phone and dialed.

"Yeah, is this the police? No, it's not an emergency. Me and my buddy are working on a house at 23 Dogwood Lane. There's a couple of stray dogs that got stuck in our Dumpster, and one of them looks vicious. Can you send someone? No, there's no hurry. They ain't going anywhere. My name? Carpenter. Carpenter by name, carpenter by trade. Okay, thanks."

He snapped his phone shut and turned to the other man.

"They said they can't get here straightaway, but that it was a good thing I called. Apparently one of their officers has already had an incident with them. They'll come and take them to the pound."

12
Narrow Escape

The two men went back into the house where they were working. Waggit was fairly certain that even though they had gone away, the reprieve was only temporary.

"We've got to find a way to get out of here," he said to Lug, who had been startled awake by the two men.

"But how?" asked Lug. "The sides are way too steep."

"Start bringing everything that you can move to this end of the Dumpster," Waggit ordered. "And let's do it quickly. We may not have much time."

Lug began to pull all the loose objects in the pile toward the end that Waggit had indicated. There were big plastic buckets that had once contained joint compound, broken planks of wood, cardboard boxes, the ends of insulation rolls, and any number of assorted items, some of which were useful, most of which weren't. As Lug dragged them to him, Waggit started to build them up against the side of the Dumpster, carefully placing items one on top of the other. He went as high as he could, and after several minutes had constructed a rather wobbly platform.

"There, that should do it," he announced. "It's not perfect, but it's tall enough for us to jump the rest."

"You can't be serious," said Lug. "Look at this body and tell me that it's able to jump the rest. In fact, look at this body and tell me that pile of junk's not going to collapse the minute I put my weight on it."

Waggit looked at Lug's chunky frame and realized that he was right.

"Okay then, here's what we do," he quickly decided.

"I'll use it to get out of here and then I'll find Felicia. She can't be far away, and she can come and get you out."

"And if you don't find her?" asked Lug nervously.

"I'll find her, don't worry," Waggit assured him.

"I *am* worried," said Lug. "You got me into this mess, and now you're just going to leave me?"

Waggit realized that the conversation was going nowhere and was taking up precious time. Now action was called for, and so he jumped onto the platform, and leapt to the top of the Dumpster with all his might. As Lug had predicted, the force of his leap caused the flimsy construction to give way, but it had given him the extra height he needed for his paws to grip the edge of the Dumpster wall. He hung on until he summoned up all his strength and pulled himself over the side, tumbling to the pavement below.

Once he was at street level he tried to get some indication as to the direction he should take. He turned his head this way and that, but there was no tingling of the nose, no communication from Felicia popping into his brain, and so he headed back the way that the two dogs had come the night before. His leash trailed behind him. He picked it up in his mouth, not just because it made running easier, but because he had seen pet dogs in the park do the same, and now was the time to look like he had an owner.

The problem was there were so many streets. He tried to cover the area as he would when hunting, but what worked in open woodland was useless in suburbia. He was beginning to panic, his chest tightening with fear, when he got the break he needed.

"Waggit, where are you? Lug, are you there?"

It was Felicia's voice in his head, so clear that she must be close to him.

"Felicia, I'm here. Where are you?"

"Waggit, where's 'here'?"

He looked around.

"I don't know, but it must be near you."

And then he turned a corner and literally bumped into her.

"Where have you been?" she asked.

"We got stuck in a Dumpster," he replied. "Lug's still in there. We have to get him out before the men come back."

Without bothering to explain how they ended up

in the Dumpster in the first place or which men were coming back, Waggit raced off with Felicia following close behind him. The problem was that he had turned down so many streets, and they all looked so similar, that he took many wrong turns before getting back to the one where Lug was trapped. His joy at finally finding the right one was shattered by the sight of an Animal Control vehicle coming up the hill, heading for the Dumpster. Although Waggit had never seen this particular truck before it was similar to the one that had taken him to the pound. He froze in fear and then shook himself back into action.

"Quick," he said to Felicia. "I have to look like a stray. Take my leash off."

She did as she was asked unquestioningly.

"Okay," said Waggit, "the Dumpster is straight up this road on the right. Go and rescue Lug and then keep going. I'll catch up with you as soon as I can."

"Be careful," she urged him. "Don't take too many risks."

How many was too many was hard to say, because if his next move went wrong the number might be one. He ran toward the truck, hidden from its occupants' view by the parked cars that lined the street.

He took cover between two of them and waited. Timing it carefully he darted out into the street just as the vehicle was upon him. The driver slammed on the brakes, causing the tires to squeal and smoke. Waggit closed his eyes and prayed that it would stop before it hit him. It finally came to a complete halt just inches from his body.

The doors flew open and a man and a woman jumped out, yelling at him. He knew then that his plan had worked. He raced across the road, narrowly avoiding a car coming in the opposite direction, with the two Animal Control officers chasing him. It was no contest. He allowed them to think that they were catching up to him for several blocks, and then he accelerated to full speed, quickly leaving them behind.

When he was sure that he had outdistanced his pursuers he slowed to a trot and caught his breath. He had bought more than enough time for Felicia to find and rescue Lug, and now the only thing left to do was for the three of them to be reunited. This proved to be easier than before, and he quickly made contact with her. She had found Lug, who was now trotting happily by her side, and the two of them were just a short distance from where Waggit was panting. When they finally caught up with one another Felicia knelt down and hugged Waggit, while Lug licked him all over his face. Since Lug's breath wasn't the sweetest Waggit had ever smelled this wasn't all that pleasant, but he appreciated the thought behind it.

"That was a very brave and silly thing to do," Felicia said to Waggit. "You could have been killed."

"Yes," agreed Waggit, "that thought occurred to me as well, but I'm still here."

"It was also very smart," Felicia said with a smile.

"Thanks, Waggit," said Lug. "You saved my life."

"S'okay," muttered Waggit. "Like you said, I was the one that got you into the mess in the first place."

"One thing I don't understand though. Why did you run when the policeman was questioning me?" asked Felicia.

"He was a Ruzela," replied Waggit. "And he might have captured us and sent us to the Great Unknown. I was scared and I panicked."

"So he panicked"—Felicia turned to Lug—"and you followed."

"Don't blame me," whined Lug, whose gratitude seemed to be short-lived. "I thought he knew what he was doing. He's always Mr. Take Charge."

"Yeah, is that so?" said Waggit, forgetting the relief he felt at Lug's rescue. "Let me tell you, I only take charge when you're so frightened you can't move, Mr. Scaredy-Pants."

"Boys! Boys!" Felicia intervened. "Let's not argue. What we have to do now is get out of here as quickly as possible. You're wanted men now, so I don't think it's a good idea to hang around."

Lug and Waggit agreed she was right, and so the three of them moved off. Waggit's desire to get away from the area was so great that he found himself pulling on his reattached leash, dragging Felicia after him.

"Waggit," she pleaded, "please slow down. Apart from the fact that I'm exhausted because I didn't get any sleep last night looking for you two miscreants, we also don't want to attract any undue attention."

An eccentrically dressed woman with a huge backpack and two mismatched dogs attracted notice anyway, especially in the suburbs through which they were passing, where anything unusual was treated with suspicion. Waggit slowed down, and they walked more slowly but without stopping. He sensed that Felicia was as eager to get out of this place as he was. When they did take a break for food or water it was for the briefest time possible. Waggit was becoming tired of the journey. His normal curiosity in his surroundings had vanished, and now he was like a horse with blinders on, focused only on the destination.

13

Home at Last

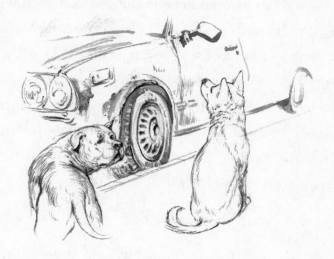

The landscape they passed through changed from big houses with large gardens to smaller ones much more crowded together. These began to be interspersed with tall apartment buildings. The streets surrounding them were lined with cars, and the number of people multiplied. The stores became more garish, with bigger, brighter signs and flashing neon lights. For Waggit this was exciting; he was beginning to feel the pulse of the city once again. But Lug, who had never seen this many people or buildings, seemed terrified. He was frightened of someone tripping over him or stepping on his paws, and he stayed as close to Felicia as possible.

It was late afternoon now, and they had been walking for many hours. They were in a neighborhood of large, drab blocks of apartments and boarded-up storefronts. Trash littered the streets, including abandoned cars, some with wheels missing and windshields smashed. Felicia suddenly stopped, took off her backpack, put it on the broken sidewalk, and sat down, her shoulders hunched in despair.

"I'm sorry, boys," she groaned. "I don't think I can go on."

"Come on, Felicia," urged Waggit. "We must be nearly there. Don't quit on us now. I so want you to meet the team and for them to know you. It's important. I want them to know that there are a few Uprights we can be friends with. We've come so far, and we're so close. We can't give up."

"That's true," said Lug, "we must go on, because I want to see trees again, and Waggit says there's lots of trees in the park."

Felicia remained slumped on the backpack. After a minute she straightened herself up.

"All right," she said. "Just let me rest for a while and then we'll continue."

"We'll look after you," Waggit assured her. "You relax and we'll protect you."

The dogs stood on either side guarding her, while she sat erect, with her eyes closed, gently breathing in and out, calming herself and restoring her strength. She had been doing this for several minutes when a car came toward them on the road. It was large and old and had obviously seen a lot of hard use. The hood was a different color from the rest of the bodywork; one of the side mirrors was held on with silver duct tape; where the radio antenna had been there was now a squashed wire coat hanger. The windows were all open, allowing the cheerful sound of loud dance music onto the dreary street. It drew next to them and stopped, and the equally cheerful face of the driver peered out of the front passenger window.

"Hey, beautiful," he cried. "What's happening?"

Felicia opened her eyes and tired though she was his smile made her smile.

"At the moment," she said with a sigh, "not much."

"Oh yeah?" the driver said. "Well, you can't stay there all day. Where you goin'?"

"Central Park," replied Felicia.

"Okay," he said. "I take you there."

"Why would you do that?" asked Felicia.

"'Cause that's what I do, lady. That's how I make my living. Look at the license plate." He chuckled. "You see what it say there? It say TLC. You know what that mean? It don' mean Tender Loving Care, believe me. It mean Taxi and Limousine Commission, and that's what I am. I am a lim-oh-zeen."

"Oh, I see." It dawned on Felicia. "You'll take us there for money?"

"That's the way I prefer it, for sure," he replied.

"How much money?" she asked.

"How about twenny?"

Felicia responded by raising her right eyebrow.

"Okay, okay," he said. "You nice lady. I take you for fifteen."

"And you don't mind the dogs?" she asked.

"Nah, I love dogs, and that's a good-looking dog." He pointed to Lug. "You wanna sell him?"

"No." Felicia smiled at the idea that anyone would pay money for Lug. "I think I'll keep him."

By now Waggit was getting restless with this conversation that he didn't understand.

"What are you talking about?" he asked Felicia.

"This man says he'll drive us to the park if we give him money," she explained.

"Do we have any?" Waggit had only a vague idea what money was.

"Enough to pay him," said Felicia.

"Can we trust him?" Waggit inquired.

"I think so," said Felicia.

Waggit didn't like the sound of *think*, but if it meant getting to the park quicker, and without having to walk anymore, it was probably worth the risk.

"Let's do it," he muttered.

"Very well," Felicia said to the man, "we accept your terms."

The driver got out and put the backpack in the trunk. He opened the rear door for Felicia and the dogs by kicking it three times while pulling hard on the handle. Felicia and Waggit got in, but Lug held back, pulling away as far as his twine leash would let him.

"It's okay," the driver said to him. "Ain't nobody gonna hurt you."

And he gently lifted the plump dog onto the backseat. He then closed the door, which involved kicking it again, and went around to the driver's seat and started the motor. The car lurched forward, leaving a trail of blue smoke in its wake. He drove very fast and had the unnerving habit of turning around to look directly at the backseat's occupants when he spoke to them. Actually he didn't speak but had to shout, because he didn't reduce the volume on the music, which, if it had been loud in the street, was deafening inside the car.

"I'm Miguel," he yelled. "What's your name?"

"Felicia," she shouted at the top of her voice.

"What?" said Miguel.

"Felicia!" she repeated even louder.

"Felicia," he said. "That's a nice name. Fel-lee-see-ya."

"Thank you," she shouted back.

"What?" he asked again.

"Do you think you could turn off the radio?" Felicia pleaded.

Miguel looked at her in the rearview mirror with an expression that indicated she had clearly lost her mind. It seemed never to have occurred to him that you could drive without constant loud music.

"Well, okay," he reluctantly agreed.

He was a man who couldn't abide silence and the

fact that his radio was switched off made him all the more talkative. He asked them where they were from, and when Felicia said upstate he told them that he loved the countryside and that in his native land he had lived as a farmer but you couldn't make any money so he joined his cousin in New York, but jobs were hard to find so he borrowed the money to buy this car and that's what he did now, seven days a week, twelve hours a day, and he liked talking to the people he picked up, but some of them made him take them places and then ran off without paying the money they owed him, and the police didn't care that a poor immigrant had just had ten dollars stolen from him because if you didn't pay your fare it was like stealing. Within a couple of miles Felicia knew all about his family, and who was talking to whom, and which one was getting married, and who just had a baby, and then suddenly he said, "Hey, there it is. Manhattan."

"Waggit, look, you're back," Felicia said.

But he was already standing up, excitedly peering over Miguel's shoulder through the windshield. There it was, glittering in the dusk, the buildings tall and sparkling, like the ones at the part of the park the dogs called the Skyline End. The car was on a raised highway heading toward this shimmering apparition.

"This is it, Lug," said Waggit. "Home."

Lug looked at it, never having seen anything like it in his life before.

"It's big, Waggit," he said. "Is it safe?"

"Stick with me and you'll be all right," Waggit replied. He was feeling so good at being back that even Lug's fear wasn't going to spoil it.

Miguel drove down an exit ramp and across a small bridge, explaining to Felicia that this way he didn't have to pay a toll, and then there they were, in the middle of it all. The cars honked, people shouted, and radios played. It was a mild night and everybody seemed to be out on the street. Lug said that it reminded him of the Fourth of July parade that came past the bar every year; in Manhattan it was just the end of an ordinary day.

They turned onto a wide avenue with trees growing in the middle and beautiful old apartment buildings on either side, in front of which stood smart, white-gloved doormen. The woman Waggit lived with before she left him at the farm also lived in an apartment building, but not one nearly as grand as these. By now Waggit could smell the park. It smelled differently from the countryside, a delicious mix of rural and city scents—fresh-cut grass mixed with exhaust fumes, new leaves competing with hotdog stands, the wind off the lake mingling with the aroma of many people. Miguel made a right turn, and then a couple of blocks later he pulled up in front of the familiar gray stone walls that marked the park's boundary.

"Here we are. This is Central Park," he said as if he owned it.

Felicia and the two dogs got out of the car, Waggit's tail vibrating with excitement. There was a moment of consternation because the trunk was stuck, trapping Felicia's backpack inside it, but after Miguel had retrieved a tire iron from beneath his seat and whacked the lid a couple of times it yawned open. From the marks on the trunk it was clear that this wasn't the first time it had been opened in this manner. Felicia got out the brown envelope in which she carried her money and extracted one ten and one five dollar bill and offered it to him.

"No," he said, "that's okay, you don't have to pay me. I like you and you dogs. You nice lady, *muy simpatico*."

"Miguel," said Felicia patiently, "I appreciate that,

but you do this for your living. You have to take the money; it wouldn't be fair to your family."

"Okay." Miguel grinned. "You *really* nice lady. Crazy, but nice. Here, I give you my card, case you need me again."

He put the money in his pocket, bid them farewell, and drove off in a cloud of smoke. When he was about two hundred feet away the radio came back on, deafening even at that distance. Felicia turned to Waggit.

"Right, Waggit. This is your park. The rest is up to you. You lead and we'll follow."

14

Team Contact

Waggit was happy to be home, even though he was uncertain of the reception he would get from the team, if there was still a team left. It was completely possible that the Ruzelas had captured every last one of them, as they had Tashi's team some time ago. Nevertheless, just being here gave him a huge surge of energy and optimism.

"It's really good to be back," he said to Felicia. "I know this place so well—every rock, every tree. There's nowhere like this."

"Unfortunately we *don't* know this place very well," she replied. "I haven't been here since I was a little girl, and Lug's never been in the park."

"I've never been in *this* park," admitted Lug, adding defensively, "but I have been in *a* park before. There was one in the town where you found me."

"Not like this one," said Waggit with pride. "This park's bigger than your whole town. This park's the best park in the world."

Since Waggit had only been in two parks in his whole life—this one and the one where the policeman had found them sleeping in the tent—his last statement was a little boastful.

"You're certainly the expert on this park," Felicia conceded, "so we're in your hands—I mean paws."

Waggit knew that if he turned to the left they would go to where the woman used to take him to play with the other pet dogs and that the path to the right would lead to the tunnel where the team lived. If they continued past that they would arrive at the Deepwoods End, which was much wilder and less visited than where they were now. So he turned right. With Felicia holding their leashes tightly they walked up the bridle path where horses came and went, and past the reservoir known to the team as the Bigwater. As they moved farther north Waggit could feel his heart quicken with excitement. Soon he would know whether or not the team would take him back. He was pulling on his leash now, with Felicia almost running to keep up with him. They rounded a corner, and there in front of them was his former home, the tunnel.

Except that it wasn't.

The structure was still there, but everything was much neater and looked a lot newer. The brush and scrubby trees that grew on top of the tunnel, and which made such a perfect place to position a sentry, were gone now, replaced by carefully mowed grass and young shrubs. The bricks of the tunnel had been spruced up as well, the missing ones replaced, and they had all been washed clean of the city soot that had built up over many years. But the most striking change was that where the entrance to the tunnel used to be there was now a sturdy wooden door painted a bright, glossy green and fastened by a huge padlock. Waggit was so shocked that he sat down, causing Lug to bang into him.

"What . . . ?" said Waggit.

"Is this the place?" asked Felicia.

"Well, it used to be," Waggit replied.

"Are you sure it's the right place?" asked Lug.

"Of course I am," said Waggit irritably. "I used to live here. I know it as well as you know the bar."

He went up to the new door, lay down, and peered through the gap at the bottom. He could just make out in the darkness what appeared to be mowing equipment, ladders, and wheelbarrows. But on the wall of the tunnel he could see the old movie poster that had adorned it when he lived there and which the workers renovating the area had not bothered to remove. So this was the right place as he had thought, but clearly it was no longer home to a pack of dogs.

"It's where we lived, all right," he said to Felicia, "but they don't live here any longer."

He stood staring at the closed door, unable to speak for a moment. To come all this way, to have endured all the dangers and discomforts of the journey, and then to be unable to find the team would be unbearable.

"Where do you think they would go if they had to move?" Felicia asked, bringing him out of his shock.

"Well," said Waggit, thinking for a moment, "they

could have gone to the Goldenside, but my guess is that they would have gone farther up into the Deepwoods. There aren't as many people there, and the woods are thicker and easier to hide in. I think that's where they would go."

"Where will *we* go?" whined Lug.

It was a good question. It was almost dark now, and as Waggit knew well, the park at night was a much more dangerous place than during the day. Not only was it easier to get lost or stumble into things that you couldn't see, there was also the added hazard of the Stoners, gangs of teenagers who often came into the park during the hours of darkness. They would terrorize both homeless people and any animals that they saw, especially dogs, throwing rocks at them and using their knives if they got close enough. They had even been known to set fires with gasoline, and one dog had died in the blaze. Why they did it nobody knew; they just seemed to enjoy wreaking havoc.

"We need somewhere safe to pitch the tent," said Felicia. "Have you any idea where that might be?"

Waggit thought hard again, his brow wrinkled with concentration. Then he remembered an area in the Deepwoods where he had once followed Tazar, the team's leader. Tazar had been spending a lot of time away from the team, and its members had been worried. Waggit had volunteered to track him and had tailed him to a small glade, surrounded by woods and with steep rocks at one end. It was there that he had seen the leader with a female dog and her two puppies. She was a loner, a stray dog who lived by herself, and Tazar was the father of her puppies. The spot where he had discovered them would make an ideal campsite. There was even a stream nearby where they could get water.

"I think I know the perfect place," he said. "Follow me."

He led them toward the Deepwoods End. They crossed the wide path the team called the Crossway, which divided the Deepwoods from the rest of the park. As soon as they were over it they were in a densely wooded area and the going became difficult, the paths narrower with tree roots waiting to trip them up and shallow gullies that were easy to stumble into. After a couple of wrong turns the path they were on suddenly opened up into the glade, now lit only by moonlight.

"Excellent," said Felicia. "You couldn't have chosen

a better location. Let's camp by the rock face."

She removed the tent from the top of her backpack and swiftly assembled it. Soon they were ready to turn in for the rest of the night, but Waggit found it difficult to sleep. He couldn't get comfortable, and his mind refused to switch off. But it was Lug, not Waggit, who heard it first—a soft rustling noise. Initially it sounded like one of the small animals that live in the park, except that instead of going in one direction, it was circling the tent.

"What do you think it is?" whispered Lug.

"I don't know," said Waggit, "but we'd better find out."

Lug didn't like the sound of "we" and let Waggit go first. Felicia was fast asleep, snoring gently like a purring cat, so Waggit took the zipper of the tent's door in his mouth and, as gently and quietly as possible, pulled it up until there was an opening big enough for the two dogs to get through. Gingerly he stuck his head out. There was nobody there that he could see, but then his nose started to twitch. It was picking up a smell, one that was very familiar to him.

"Cal?" he said.

There was silence, and then a slight rustling

followed by a whispered, "Waggit? Is that you?"

"It is, Cal," said Waggit. "It is me."

"Who's with you?" the voice asked.

"Another dog called Lug," said Waggit, "and a female Upright called Felicia."

There was a pause.

"An Upright? Is she okay?"

"She's more okay than any Upright you've ever met," said Waggit. "Or me, for that matter."

There was another period of silence, and then out of a bush at the edge of the woods a dog cautiously appeared. He was of medium build, still young, and with German Shepherd somewhere in his background. When Waggit saw him he gave a yelp of joy, then ran over to him, tail wagging with delight, and licked his face effusively. The other dog seemed equally pleased to see Waggit and buried his nose in the fur at the back of his neck. Lug stood nervously on the sidelines, not quite sure what he was supposed to do.

"It's good to see you again," said Waggit.

"You too," said Cal. "When did you get back?"

"Just this rising," said Waggit. "I went straight to the tunnel, but it had all changed. What happened?"

"Oh, it was awful," said Cal. "One day some

Uprights came, not Ruzelas, but the ones that work with them. They started to take all of the boxes and stuff out of the tunnel, and others cut down the trees and bushes on top. Fortunately we was all out when it happened, except for Alicia, but she managed to get away. You know how fast she is. But there we were, homeless, like a bunch of loners. I tell you, Waggit, I think Uprights are taking over the world."

It was at this point that Felicia chose to come out of the tent. When he saw her, Cal backed away, hackles up.

"It's okay, really," said Waggit. "This is Felicia. Felicia, this is Cal. He's one of my old teammates."

"I'm very pleased to meet you, Cal," said Felicia politely.

Cal tipped his head to one side inquisitively. Then he sidled up to Waggit and whispered in his ear.

"Is it my imagination, or can she understand what we say?"

"She sure can," confirmed Waggit. "I told you that you've never met an Upright like her."

"And she can speak to us as well?" Cal asked.

"She does," Waggit assured him.

"My word," Cal said.

"Your every word, actually," said Waggit.

There was a whimper from the sidelines.

"Oh, I'm sorry," said Waggit. "This is Lug."

Cal had been so focused on Waggit that he hadn't even noticed the pit bull.

"Is he all right?" he asked Waggit.

"Well," said Waggit, "I wouldn't say that exactly, but he's not like you think he is. If he ever summoned the courage to fight his own shadow it would probably win."

"He looks a lot like Tashi," Cal observed, "only fatter, of course."

Tashi was the team's archenemy, a violent and treacherous dog with a love of fighting, and fighting dirty at that.

"He doesn't act like Tashi," said Waggit. "It might be better if he did."

Lug lay down with his head on his paws and sighed.

"I'm convinced he has many other fine qualities," Felicia interjected. "We just don't know what they are yet."

This didn't seem to cheer Lug up at all. Cal, for his

part, remained suspicious of Felicia. He looked at her with a mixture of fear and awe until she began to talk to him in what Waggit now thought of as her calming voice.

"Now, Cal, I overheard you telling Waggit the sad story of losing your home. It's a terrible thing to be without shelter or a place to call you own."

Waggit thought this an odd thing for a woman to say who, as far as he knew, had no home other than the tent they were standing in front of.

"Tell me," she continued, "has the team found somewhere else to live?"

"Yes," said Cal with a dreamy look on his face that was a sure indication he was under her spell.

"And where is it?" she asked.

"It's right under your tent," Cal replied.

15
Welcomed Back

They all looked at the tent as if expecting to see a steady stream of dogs coming out of its entrance. But as Cal explained, the team's new home was beneath the campsite. They had discovered it after a very heavy rainstorm one night. Rainwater had carved a deep gully around the roots of a tree and had revealed the top of a large sewage pipe below the surface. It was broken and no longer worked, and after some concerted digging by the larger members of the team, an entrance was made that allowed the dogs to crawl inside.

"It's good from a security point of view," said Cal, "but it's not really big enough and gets very stuffy when we're all in there. In fact on warm nights a lot of us sleep outside, but it's better than nothing, which is what we had before we found it."

From his description Waggit realized that this was a far cry from the spacious safety of the tunnel, and it was upsetting to think of his friends living in such reduced circumstances. He wondered why things had to change all the time; what harm would it do if they stayed the same? None that he could see.

Cal looked at Felicia. "Is this the woman what adopted you?" he asked.

"No," said Waggit. "I met Felicia upstate."

"We've been traveling together," Felicia explained.

"Where's upstate?" asked Cal, who had not been outside the park since he was abandoned there at a young age.

"Oh, it's a long way away," said Waggit with all the experience of a world traveler. "Farther than you could imagine."

"How did you get there?" asked Cal.

"The woman who adopted me took me to a farm and left me there. It was horrible," he said.

"Well, that's Uprights for you," declared Cal. "Even the so-called good ones you can't trust."

"We don't know that exactly," Felicia interrupted. "We don't know if she left you there for good. She may have intended to come and collect you at some point."

Waggit and Cal looked at each other and rolled their eyes, but both let her comment pass without a response.

"So what're you going to do now?" asked Cal.

"I was hoping the team would take me back," said Waggit. "Do you think they will?"

"I would," Cal assured him, "and I'm sure all the others would as well, but really it's up to Olang."

"Olang?" asked Waggit.

"You remember," said Cal. "Tazar's son, Olang. Tazar won't do nothing now without Olang says it's okay."

Waggit remembered that he had met Olang once when the dog was a puppy. He was an unremarkable creature who was quite aggressive even then, but Tazar clearly adored him.

"When can I see everybody again?" asked Waggit.

"Well," said Cal, "I've got to go, because I'm supposed to be on eyes and ears, but why don't we all get together first thing in the rising?"

It was agreed that Cal would tell the team about Waggit's return and bring them to the tent at daybreak. Then they parted, Cal back to his sentry duty and the other three to the tent to get some sleep. Waggit nodded off almost immediately, only to awaken a few hours later with a start. He could feel the presence of dogs all around him, and he knew that Cal had been as good as his word. He opened the flap of the tent and looked outside.

There they were, the whole team, waiting to see him: Cal, Raz, Lady Alicia, Lady Magica, Lady Alona, Gruff, Gordo, Little One, and Little Two. As he came out of the tent they crowded around him, tails wagging, everyone trying to lick his face or nuzzle into his fur. The air was filled with growls of approval and howls of welcome, and Waggit could feel relief flooding through his body.

His fears had proven to be groundless. This was his family, his tribe, the animals he felt closest to in the world. Magica told him how much she missed him, and Gordo said that it was good to have the best hunter back because the food supply had been somewhat stingy of late. Even Gruff, the grouch of the group, said that he supposed he was quite pleased to see him, probably.

Alicia, a long-limbed, purebred Afghan hound, grudg-ingly said that if they had to have someone else in the cramped quarters in which they now lived then it might as well be someone as skinny as him.

Suddenly the excitement quieted down and the dogs moved apart to reveal Tazar, the leader, tall and dig-nified, with his shiny black coat and magnificent tail that he carried proudly like a battle standard. Waggit noticed that he had a few gray hairs on his muzzle, but these seemed to make him look even more distin-guished than before.

"Waggit, my friend." His voice boomed. "Welcome back. We never expected you to come back once, let alone twice."

After the woman had rescued him from the pound Waggit had returned to tell the team he was safe and living with her.

Now he looked Tazar in the eyes.

"This time, Tazar," he said respectfully, "I would like to stay, if the team will have me, of course."

"Waggit, you're our family, our brother," Tazar replied. "Family doesn't abandon one of its own just because he makes a mistake. We're only canine, after all."

"Not so fast, Pa," said a voice behind Tazar. "How do you know he's not a spy for the Uprights, sent to find out where we are? He's been living with Uprights, so how do we know if we can still trust him?"

The owner of the voice moved next to Tazar, and Waggit saw a large, muscled dog with narrow, mean eyes. He was black except for a large white patch over one eye that made him look even more sinister. This was Olang, the leader's son.

"My boy," said Tazar, "if it was anyone else, your question would have been well put. But this is Waggit, and if nothing else he is honorable. He may have been foolish at times, but I would trust him with my life."

"Well, I think you're too soft with some of these strays." Olang continued, "We can't just take in anyone that comes along. It isn't fair to the rest of us."

Waggit hurriedly tried to change the topic of conversation.

"I don't see Lowdown. Has he, I mean is he, well, you know, did he die?"

"Well, let's see," said Tazar. "You know, I'm not sure. Why don't we ask him? Lowdown, did you die yet?"

There was a wheezing chuckle from the edge of the glade.

"Not yet, Tazar, but I might by the time I get to you."

Waggit turned in the direction of the voice to see a scruffy, short-legged, and very old dog slowly and painfully moving toward them. It was Lowdown. Waggit had been closer to this aged creature than any other animal, and with a yelp of pleasure he ran over to him.

"Lowdown, you're still here," he cried with joy in his voice.

"Yup," agreed Lowdown, "it's a miracle, ain't it? I guess I must be tougher than I thought." He paused. "Or maybe just more stubborn."

"And who would this be?" asked Tazar.

Waggit turned around to see Lug, who had finally ventured out of the tent and now stood there shaking with fear at the sight of so many dogs.

"This is Lug," replied Waggit.

"Glad to know you, Lug," boomed Tazar. "Any friend of Waggit's is welcome here."

"Well, he's not exactly a friend," said Waggit. "We rescued him from some Uprights who were trying to stone him to death. He just sort of tagged along after that."

"Ah," said Tazar in his wisest tone of voice. "The Uprights, the perfidious Uprights."

Tazar sometimes used words that nobody knew. Whether *he* knew what they meant was something else that nobody knew.

"And talking of Uprights," he continued, "Cal tells me that you're traveling in the company of one with remarkable powers."

"I am," replied Waggit, "and without her I probably wouldn't have made it back."

He stuck his head inside the tent.

"Felicia," he said, "come and meet the team."

Felicia unfolded her long body from inside the tent. She was an imposing sight when she stood up to her full height, but this time Waggit could feel she was trying hard to make her aura of peace as strong as she possibly could. As a result most of the team members moved toward her out of curiosity, something they would never have done with any other human being. Only one, Olang, pulled back, growling softly.

"It's a pleasure to meet you all," she said in the softest of voices. "My name is Felicia. I know how important you all are to Waggit, and now that I see you I understand why."

The team seemed pleased to hear this, and none of them appeared to be surprised that she could understand them and they her, so Waggit assumed that Cal had already told them of her ability to communicate with dogs.

"He has especially spoken of you, Tazar," she continued, "and how you are both his hero and his mentor."

Upon hearing this Tazar puffed up with pride so that he looked even bigger and sleeker than ever.

"Well, I try to keep them all on the right path, but sometimes they stray," he said modestly. "Waggit's one of my favorites. I think of him as a son."

This clearly did not go down very well with Olang, who growled and bared his teeth. "I can't believe what I'm seeing and hearing," he said. "You always told me that Uprights are the enemy, and there isn't such a thing as a good Upright, and here you are chatting away with one like she was one of us. It's not right."

With that he turned tail and disappeared into the woods.

"You must excuse my boy," said Tazar to Felicia. "He's a good dog, but he has strong opinions about most things, and it's true that I usually make sure that none of the team goes near an Upright. But we've never met one like you before."

"There's no need to apologize," said Felicia graciously. "I feel honored that you're prepared to make an exception for me, and you will find that I will never betray your trust."

"No," concurred Tazar, "I have an instinct that you won't. In the meantime you'd better pack up that cloth house of yours. Even though this is the Deepwoods, the Ruzelas still come around here sometimes, and I'll guarantee they won't let you keep it there."

Felicia agreed, and started to collect her possessions, such as they were, and to roll up the tent. When she had done this they all stood around in an embarrassed silence, as if not knowing what to do next. Gordo broke the hush.

"We would invite you all to breakfast," he said, "only we don't have any."

"We had some delicious scurry what I hunted yesterday," Raz told Felicia, "but it's all gone."

"What exactly is scurry?" inquired Felicia.

"You know," said Cal, "those small creatures with long tails. There's lots of them in the park. You'd've loved the ones Raz caught."

"I'm sure I would," Felicia replied, although Waggit

could tell from her voice that she was sure she wouldn't. There was another awkward pause, and then she said, "Is there anywhere that I could put our things so that they won't be seen until we can find somewhere better for the tent?"

This caused a lot of frowns of concentration, scratching of itches, and smacking of lips, all of which indicated that the dogs were giving the problem their finest thinking.

"What about . . . ?"

"No."

"Maybe under . . . ?"

"Too open."

"Hanging on . . . ?"

"You could see it."

For each dog who had a suggestion there was another to shoot it down until Alona, the shiest dog on the team, said, "Well, I'm sure this isn't a very good idea, but at the back of Half Top Hill there's a place where three big rocks come together, and in the middle they form a kind of chimney. The stuff would be out of sight there, only it's always a bit wet."

"That doesn't matter," said Felicia. "The tent and the backpack are both waterproof. It sounds like a perfect place. Come and show me where it is."

Alona was shocked that her suggestion had been accepted and even more surprised that she was needed as a guide. The two of them went off in the direction of the hill looking just like any other woman and her dog out for an early morning walk, although both were a little stranger than most.

Waggit looked around at the assorted dogs surrounding him. Although he had never been fonder of anyone, there was something different about them, an unease that he hadn't felt before. Was it his return that was causing this? If the team was uncomfortable with his homecoming, then he had no home, whatever Tazar had said. The whole point of a team was that its members all worked together; if they didn't it would fall apart.

"Is everything okay?" he asked.

"Oh, sure, fine," said Raz.

"Are you all right with me rejoining the team?" Waggit continued, believing that it was better to get this out in the open from the very start.

There was a general murmur of approval, which was reassuring. If it wasn't him, then what else could be causing this awkwardness?

"Do you have a problem with Lug here?" Waggit continued. "He doesn't have anywhere else to go."

"No," said Magica. "He's fine."

"Well, what is it, then?" said Waggit, getting frustrated now.

"Oh, nothing," mumbled Little One.

Tazar interrupted the awkward conversation.

"You're welcome. You're both welcome," he said. "So no more of this nonsense. I've got to go and see where my wayward son's gotten to, but you all work out sleeping arrangements and duties and so on. I'll see you later."

He headed off into the woods, leaving the rest of the team standing around Waggit. The silence continued. Waggit turned toward Lowdown. He knew from experience that he would get the truth from him.

"Okay, Lowdown," he said. "What's the problem?"

Lowdown took a deep breath.

"Well, in a word," he said, "Olang."

16
Felicia's Feast

It was as if Lowdown had let a cork out of a bottle. It seemed that each dog had a story about Olang that they were dying to tell but had been too frightened to reveal until now—tales of his bullying and arrogance, and the way that he lied to Tazar, spreading false rumors, and taking credit for kills that someone else had hunted.

"I think he's horrid," said Lady Magica, who was the kindest of dogs and never had a bad word for anyone.

"He ain't just horrid," Lady Alicia complained. "He's ugly and he smells bad."

This was the worst thing she could say about anyone.

"It's worse than that, Waggit," said Gordo, who was part Labrador and constantly overweight. "I once caught him hiding food for himself instead of sharing it with the rest of the team, like we are supposed to. He said that if I ever told anyone he would bite my tongue off while I slept, and then I'd never be able to eat again."

The thought of this sent a shudder through Gordo's ample body. It was a threat he had taken seriously, because, as everyone knew, Gordo slept with his tongue hanging out.

Waggit suddenly realized that the reason they were all talking about these things now was that they were looking to him to do something about the situation, but what he was not quite sure.

"If you're all so upset about Olang, why don't you say something to Tazar about him?" he asked.

"Tazar's a great dog and a fine leader," said Lowdown. "He's kept this team together through some difficult times, as you know, but like most great dogs he has a blind spot, and his is Olang. He won't hear nothing bad said about him, and everything the miserable cur says is like law to Tazar. If he said hot was cold Tazar would believe him."

There was a chorus of agreement.

"If you say anything that is even a little bit critical of him," said Raz, "he comes back and tells Tazar the most awful lies about you, and even if you've got a dozen witnesses what says you didn't do the thing he says you did, Tazar don't believe you."

"And he's the most awful bully," said Little One. "He's always pushing Little Two around and snapping at him."

"It's true," said Little Two shamefacedly.

"So what are you going to do about it?" asked Waggit.

There was an awkward silence again.

"Well," said Lowdown eventually, "we was hoping you would have a talk with Tazar about it. He always had a soft spot for you, and he listens to what you say. Can't you tell him that you noticed how unhappy we are, and how we talked about it? If you do it straight-away he'll know that it ain't because you've got a grumble against Olang, but because you're worried about the team sticking together."

The team breaking up was exactly what Waggit was worried about. If this went on unchecked it could split the dogs into two groups, with Tazar and Olang on one side, and the rest of the dogs on the other. Although there were many fine animals on the team, they needed a leader, and as far as Waggit could see, there was nobody among them who could take the place of Tazar. What Lowdown said made a lot of sense, but the thought of confronting Tazar about anything, least of all his illusions about his son, was very scary; even though he was a great dog, he had a fearsome temper. On the other hand, if the team broke up Waggit would truly be homeless, and this was something that was even more frightening than facing Tazar.

"Okay," he said hesitantly. "I'll do it—when the time is right."

"Don't leave it too long though," warned Lowdown. "The sooner the better."

"I know," replied Waggit.

A surge of relief went through the group when they heard him agree to do this. It was as if the problem was already solved. Although this was gratifying, it didn't make the task any easier.

"Come on, Waggit," said Cal, "let's show you the pipe so that you can choose where you want to sleep. There's not much room, though, I warn you."

Lug coughed gently behind them.

"Oh, yeah, you can come too," said Cal. "I guess if Gordo can get through the entrance you can. I don't think we'll ever fit Felicia in though."

His last comment caused a ripple of chuckles to go through the team.

Cal led them past the place where the tent had been to a big, old maple tree at the foot of a rocky incline. From the side that they were approaching it looked like any other tree in the park, but when Waggit got between it and the rocks he could see a hole in the ground between its roots. It certainly didn't look big enough for a dog of Gordo's stature to get through, but according to Cal he used it frequently, although always accompanied by much groaning and panting.

Cal went first, followed by Raz, and then Waggit prepared to push himself inside. Before he did he turned to see whether or not Lug was following. He was standing several feet back.

"S'okay," Lug said. "You go ahead. I'll stay here,

sort of stand guard. Tell me what it's like."

Waggit shrugged, turned toward the hole, and disappeared down it. In the darkness it was impossible to see where he was going, and suddenly he felt the ground drop away from beneath his feet and he tumbled down to find himself on the floor of the pipe. Now that he wasn't blocking the light with his body and his eyes had become accustomed to the gloom, he could see his surroundings better.

While the pipe was large for a pipe, it was a small place for dogs to live in. Waggit couldn't see how Alicia would be able to stand up in it to her full height. In fact he was pretty sure she couldn't. It had obviously been part of a drainage system, of which there were many in this part of the park, where streams ran into pools and small ponds. The pipe had fallen into disuse when it fractured in two places, one where the dogs entered it, and another about twenty feet along where earth had trickled down over the years and now completely blocked it, cutting off any possibility of escape.

The only light came through the shallow entry tunnel, and what it illuminated was not good. Because the floor of the pipe was round, an attempt had been made to flatten it with newspapers and cardboard boxes. Many of these were wrinkled where water had come into the pipe, presumably from the entrance. They were also filthy, and Waggit remembered how scrupulous Tazar had been about keeping the tunnel clean and how frequently he had insisted that they remove all the cardboard boxes and paper on which they slept and replace them with fresh ones. The air in the pipe was damp and stale and smelled strongly of its occupants.

"This is another thing that Olang took credit for," Cal said. "There was four of us what found the pipe, and he was just one of them, but he ran off and told Tazar about it first so that it looked like he found it all by himself."

"Why is it so dirty?" asked Waggit. "Doesn't Tazar say anything?"

"Oh, it drives him nuts," replied Cal. "But it's really hard to get boxes and clean paper in the pipe and the old stuff out and, to be honest with you, everyone's so fed up we can't be bothered. Olang tells Tazar it's 'cause we're lazy, but it ain't. It's 'cause we ain't got any enthusiasm for it."

"Why didn't you say something to Tazar about the effect Olang's having on the team?" asked Waggit.

"You don't seem to understand," said Raz, with an edge of frustration in his voice. "You can't say *anything* to Tazar that puts Olang in a bad light. He just don't want to know about it."

Just then the pipe went dark, and they all looked up to see the unmistakable silhouette of the leader looking down from the entry.

"Well, what d'you think?" Tazar asked Waggit. "Pretty good, eh? Warm, secure, easily defended. My boy found it, you know. Mind you, it needs tidying up a bit, although nobody except for Olang and myself seems to be bothered by that."

"Tazar," said Waggit, summoning up all his courage, "can you and I talk?"

"Sure we can," said Tazar. "You know me. I've always got time for a team member. Come on up."

Waggit scrambled back through the hole, shook the dirt from his coat, and had reached Tazar when Felicia's voice pierced through the glade.

"Okay, everybody, come and get it."

Tazar and Waggit turned to see her tall figure laden down with shopping bags, Alona trotting proudly by her side wearing the expression of one who knows a secret.

"Now listen up," Felicia declared in her most authoritative voice. "I don't have enough money to do this every day, but I thought that we should celebrate Waggit's return to the team with a special breakfast."

The dogs had gathered around, curious to discover what she had in the bags. She opened them up and started to retrieve the most amazing assortment of food that they had ever seen. Even Olang, who had returned after sulking in the woods for a while, moved forward in curiosity. From the deli there was salami and roast beef, hot dogs and different cheeses, and from the pet store there were rawhide chews, smoked pigs' ears, and large, crunchy biscuits. As the contents of each package was laid out on the ground all Gordo could say was, "Oh my! Oh my!"

The feast was magnificent, and even Magica's sensible suggestion that maybe they should save some for a later date was swept aside. This was a celebration, a homecoming; it was not a time to be practical. Tazar took over the distribution of the food and the seating arrangements, and Felicia was wise enough to let him. When all was in place, and each dog sat in front of a pile of food and other goodies, Tazar intoned the prayer that he said every time the dogs ate:

"Remember as you eat, you eat your brother's food; remember as you sleep, you take your sister's space; remember as you live, your life belongs to them. You are the team; the team is you. The two are one; the one is two."

That said, nothing much else was, for the serious task of eating good food demanded utmost concentration. Felicia was given the honor of sitting between Tazar and Waggit. Lowdown sat on Waggit's left, and Olang on Tazar's right.

"The food is fine, Felicia," Tazar said between mouthfuls. "It really is fine."

"So is your team, Tazar," Felicia graciously replied.

And indeed, for that moment it did seem as if they were. Waggit looked around at them enjoying themselves and their meal, and the conversations he had such a short time ago seemed to have been with a different pack of dogs. This was the old team, close-knit, fun-loving, a family.

Tazar turned to Waggit.

"You wanted to say something to me?" he asked.

"Later," said Waggit. "It can wait till later. For now let's just enjoy ourselves."

17
Lowdown's Hideaway

It took the team only a short time to finish the meal. The dogs who had the good sense not to overeat—and believe it or not there were a couple—took their pigs' ears or rawhide chews off to secret spots to be buried and dug up later. This was not an option open to those who had been seated next to Alicia, whose appetite was legendary.

"If you ain't gonna eat that," she was heard to shriek, "I'll finish it up for you."

And without waiting for an answer from the food's

unfortunate owner, she did just that. The two big mysteries of life in the park were how Alicia stayed so thin no matter how much she ate, and how Gordo never lost an ounce, even in the leanest times when the dogs might go for days without food.

The next order of business, after the licking and belching that generally followed a meal, was what to do with Felicia. While it was true that she had money, it was not enough for her to stay in any but the most modest of hotels, and furthermore she had an aversion to sleeping in buildings. The problem was, of course, that apart from the park there were very few open spaces in the city where you could pitch a tent—actually, none.

At Tazar's suggestion the team broke up into several groups to search the area in the general vicinity of the pipe for suitable locations where the tent would be hidden from view. As was usually the case, Gruff stayed behind, claiming a frailty that no one else could see. Lowdown remained for the same reason, only in his case the frailty was apparent to everyone. Lady Alicia refused to join the search, regarding such activities, or indeed any activity that benefited the common good, as being beneath the dignity of a purebred dog.

Waggit went with Cal and Raz, whose company he always enjoyed, and Lug tagged along as well; Gordo lumbered off with Magica, whom he had adored forever, and whom he would have followed anywhere; they were joined by Little One and Little Two, to whom Magica had been like a mother; Tazar and Olang left with the air of dogs who had important business to discuss.

It was Alona and Felicia who found the perfect place. Because Alona had been a loner, which was how she got her name, she knew the Deepwoods End better than anyone. She was also skilled at finding hiding places, a necessity for dogs who lived without the protection of a team. In fact she herself had used the spot to which she took Felicia as a refuge. It was at the foot of a tall, elegant willow tree growing next to a stream. A cascade of long, trailing branches almost touched the ground and became intertwined with rushes that grew around the stream's edge. Between them the tree and the grasses formed a natural tent, which would almost completely hide Felicia's. When Alona was sure that her companion was satisfied with the choice she gave out one long and three short, low howls, loud enough for the rest of the team to hear, but not so loud as to attract the attention of any humans who might be in the area.

Soon the other Tazarians gathered around and expressed their approval of the location. Felicia was so excited with the discovery that she wanted to get the tent as soon as possible and erect it on its new site, so she and Alona went to retrieve it from the rocks where they had hidden it just a few short hours ago. The other team members wandered off after agreeing to return to help with any extra camouflage that might be necessary when the tent was in position, and for the first time since returning to the park Waggit found himself alone—well, almost alone, because he still had Lug, his inevitable shadow. They trotted off along a narrow wooded path in the direction of the meadow.

"Where are we going?" asked Lug.

"Back to the pipe," Waggit replied tersely.

"Are you going to sleep there tonight?" Lug inquired with anxiety in his voice.

"Dunno yet."

"I hope not. It looks spooky to me," said Lug.

Secretly Waggit agreed with him. The thought of spending the night in that stuffy, claustrophobic tube was not something that held any appeal for him, despite the fact that he wanted to be close to his old teammates. He wasn't going to admit this to Lug, however, and so the pair of them proceeded in silence. It was a few minutes later when they literally bumped into Tazar. The path they were on converged with another, but the undergrowth was so high, and Waggit was so preoccupied with the team's problems, that he didn't notice the leader on the other path until they collided with each other. Tazar must have been deep in thought also, because both dogs were startled by the sudden appearance of the other, and both raised their hackles and growled.

"Oh, Waggit," said Tazar. "It's you." Then he noticed Lug behind Waggit. "And—er, what's his name again?"

"Lug," replied Waggit.

"Lug, yes, absolutely right," said Tazar in a tone of voice that seemed to indicate he was testing Waggit to see whether *he* remembered the other dog's name. "That's an interesting Upright you brought us," he continued, "really interesting. Never met one like her."

"Well," said Waggit, "so far she's really been great.

I don't think I would've made it back without her. I trust her."

"Hmm." Tazar was skeptical. "I'm not sure I would go that far. She's unusual, I'll give you that, but she's still an Upright. When the paw meets the pavement they look after each other before they concern themselves with us, but she's different enough from all the others to give her the benefit of the doubt. I guess time will tell. And talking about time, how long do you think she's going to be around?"

"She's a wanderer," said Waggit. "I get the impression she doesn't like to stay too long in any one place, so I don't know exactly, but I wouldn't think it'll be forever."

"What about the team?" asked Tazar, changing the subject abruptly. "I'm worried about them. They seem so morose much of the time, and I can't understand why."

Waggit drew in a deep breath. His heart was pounding with fear, but circumstances would never be better than this to start the conversation the team was relying on him to have with Tazar.

"Well . . . you know, um," he said hesitantly, "I

haven't really been around long enough—well, actually, um, not long at all—to help you with that one—although perhaps they do seem a little down."

"Well, I'd appreciate your thoughts," said Tazar, "when you zero in on what the problem is." He looked at the length of the shadows cast by the trees. "Great Vinda, is that the time? I must be off. Let's talk later."

As he disappeared into the undergrowth Waggit felt wretched that he hadn't taken advantage of the opportunity to bring up the subject of Olang. It wasn't just that he was scared of Tazar's reaction, although he was. But now that he thought about it more it seemed that he hadn't been around long enough. There was always the possibility that the team was blaming Olang for things that weren't his fault—the restricted living conditions in the pipe, for example. Waggit didn't yet know if their determined dislike of the dog was justified, and until he saw for himself how Olang behaved he would withhold judgment. It was a serious matter to come between a father and his son.

"I thought you wanted to talk to Tazar about Olang," said Lug, whom Waggit had completely forgotten was there.

"I'll do it later," replied Waggit.

"Suit yourself," said Lug, "but that seemed as good a time as any."

Waggit decided at that moment that Lug was even more irritating when he was right than when he was cowardly.

Later that afternoon they all stood around the willow tree trying to see where Felicia's tent was, but the camouflage work that they themselves had done, as well as the natural characteristics of the location, made it impossible to spot. Of course to a dog its scent gave away its position, but their experience with humans was that the poor things had virtually no sense of smell and equally inadequate hearing. Their sight didn't seem to be that great either, and so the dogs felt fairly confident that Felicia would be in no danger, from her own kind at least. Despite the fact that Felicia was human, the whole team seemed to be excited about helping her. Once again Waggit saw how easily they worked together and how strong the bonds were among them. All except Olang, who sulked or made disparaging remarks about the foolishness of dogs who allowed themselves to be duped by humans.

It was an echo of his father, only meaner and angrier.

When night fell Waggit decided that he would sleep with the team in the pipe. This was not because he wanted to; he would have infinitely preferred to be with Felicia in the safety of her hidden tent. But he felt that if he was truly rejoining the team he had to live with them from the outset and share the discomforts that they suffered. He was also somewhat worried by Olang's comments about humans, especially when he'd implied that Waggit was a spy for the Uprights and shouldn't be trusted. The fact that he had left the team once to go with a human and now had returned in the company of another could be fertile ground for suspicion, and he felt he had to prove his loyalty to his teammates.

He settled into the confined space of the pipe. He hadn't realized just how cramped it was until he tried to find enough room to lie down, in the end nestling between Gordo's outstretched legs, his head resting on that dog's ample stomach. The temperature in the pipe soon became significantly higher than outside and the air was filled with the sound of tongues panting, as well as Gordo's snores. Waggit was hot and restless;

he couldn't get comfortable and found himself wishing that he was Lug, who didn't have to prove himself to anyone. Because of this the pit bull was now blissfully stretched out next to Felicia in the coolness of her tent.

After about half an hour of tossing and turning, none of which disturbed Gordo's slumbers, Waggit decided to go out for some fresh air, and maybe join Little One and Little Two, who were on sentry duty that night. Normally only one dog would be on eyes and ears, but these two never did anything without the other. Waggit stepped as carefully as he could around the other dogs in the pipe, although even with his vigilance he still managed to provoke a few growls on the way out. He finally scrambled up the entry tunnel and into the cool night air. He took several lungfuls that tasted as sweet as cool, fresh water, shook himself, was about to go and find the sentries when he heard a wheezing chuckle behind him.

"Heh, heh. Too friendly for comfort down there?" inquired Lowdown.

"Well, it *is* a bit cramped," admitted Waggit.

"And a bit warm, I'll bet."

"How come you're not in the pipe?"

"With my legs!" exclaimed Lowdown. "I'd have to get Cal or Raz or another of those strong boys to carry me in and out like a puppy, and I'm way too old to be a puppy. No, they know I don't sleep there. What they don't know is where I do. Come, follow me."

Lowdown hobbled off painfully, with Waggit following closely behind. They had gone some distance from the pipe's entrance when they came upon a large, dead oak tree, most of its branches missing, with ivy all over its trunk and ferns growing at its base. Lowdown walked straight up to it and pushed some of the foliage aside with his nose to reveal that the tree had a completely hollow trunk. Into this the short brown dog had pulled some cardboard and newspaper, and now had a safe, cool, and comfortable spot to spend each night.

"Home," said Lowdown. "And my house is your house."

Waggit looked at his generous friend and a wave of affection flooded over him. He began to lick the old fellow all over his face.

"Hey, hey, enough of that," spluttered Lowdown. "You know I don't hold with too much washing."

"That's not washing," said Waggit. "That's love!"

"Yeah, well," Lowdown grumbled. "Whatever it is ain't going to get us a good night's sleep."

Then they settled down to rest.

18
Olang's Challenge

Waggit woke up with a start the next day, disoriented and confused. Once again he was in a strange place, as he had been on so many mornings recently. It seemed it was something he would never get used to, and it wasn't until he heard Lowdown's gentle snoring and turned to see his friend beside him that he began to relax. The hollow of the tree trunk was not big, but it was cool and dry, and a soft green light filtered through the leaves of the ferns that concealed its opening. As he lay there a sense of calm and peace began to wash over him, relaxing muscles that were still stiff from the night's sleep. He was content.

The only place I've ever been that I feel like this, he thought, is here in the park with Lowdown and the others.

If he had reflected a bit harder he would have remembered that he had also been this content in the woman's apartment and with the dogs who lived in the same building. He was so angry with her for abandoning him at the farm that he wouldn't allow himself to remember the good times they had, nor dwell on the fact that he owed his life to her just as much as to Tazar and the team. If she had not come along in the nick of time and rescued him from the pound he would have met the same fate that awaited most of its inmates.

But these memories were the farthest thing from his mind on this warm summer morning. He was content to let his body absorb his surroundings, smelling the scent of the earth and feeling a soft breeze ruffle the hair of his coat. A dove cooed gently and was then drowned out by the more insistent *rat-a-tat* of a woodpecker, and underlying all these sounds was the hum of the traffic that never seemed to stop. A sudden early morning itch developed behind his right ear that needed scratching immediately, and in doing so he woke up Lowdown. The old dog yawned, his long pink tongue with its purple patch looking much too big for his mouth. He groaned softly as he stretched his ancient limbs.

"Why is it you youngsters have to get up so early?" he asked, pretending to be grumpy.

"Well, somebody has to go out and provide for you old guys," teased Waggit, "'cause I don't see you hunting too often."

The old dog laughed.

"You got that right," he said. "My hunting days were never filled with glory at the best of times. Now my aching old body can barely make it to the stream for a good drink of water."

"I'm sorry to see you like this," said Waggit, now serious.

"Don't be," said Lowdown. "The way I am now is the result of living a long time. It's better than the alternative, let me tell you. And for the most part it's been a good life too."

"Is it still?" Waggit asked.

Lowdown thought for a moment.

"Yes," he said after careful consideration, "I would

say so. The team looks after me well, and I ain't got no complaints. It ain't like it used to be, but then nothing is."

"What's the difference?" asked Waggit.

"The dogs are more scared," Lowdown replied. "They ain't as open with each other as they was, especially when that brat Olang's around. You can't say nothing in front of him without him going to Tazar and telling him what you said, only making it sound much worse. You certainly can't joke around in front of him; he don't know what a joke is, and it's sad, 'cause we all used to have so much fun."

Both dogs fell silent. Waggit had already experienced the unease that he described. He knew that the old dog thought Waggit was the only animal who could do anything about it, but he wasn't so sure. Why would Tazar pay any attention to him after he had betrayed everything the leader believed in when he left to live with the woman?

"Well, even though it ain't the team it used to be," Lowdown said, interrupting the other's thoughts, "it's still the team, and we'd better go and see what it's up to today."

"Lead on, old friend," said Waggit.

"Happy to," replied Lowdown. "Just don't expect any speed records to be broken between here and there."

When they arrived at the pipe they found the team assembled, and in a strange mood. The dogs were all quiet and clearly uncomfortable. They barely responded to Waggit's cheerful greetings and avoided making eye contact with him. Only Olang seemed at ease, strutting around the group with his tail up and his ears pricked.

"Something's happening," Lowdown whispered in Waggit's ear, "and Olang's behind whatever it is."

Olang saw the two of them and swaggered up.

"Why, Waggit," he sneered, "I didn't notice you sleeping in the pipe last night. Didn't want to get too doggie, maybe? Spent the night with your Upright friend, did you?"

Lowdown stepped between Waggit and Olang.

"He slept where I slept," he said to Olang.

"And where would that be?" Olang asked.

"None of your business," replied Lowdown.

"We know you're too old and decrepit to get into the pipe," taunted Olang, "so we overlook what you do, but if Waggit wants to come back to the team he has to be a part of everything *we* do, unless, of course, he feels too grand for us with his precious Upright ways."

"If I felt too grand," said Waggit, trying to be as calm as possible, "why would I have come back here in the first place? No, I don't feel too good to come back to the team, but I feel good enough."

"Well, you're not good enough in my eyes," replied Olang, who turned and walked away.

None of the other dogs said anything during this exchange. Whatever feelings they had were put on hold with the appearance of Tazar, who jumped agilely onto a nearby rock so that all could see him. As he did this Olang sidled up beside him, a smug expression on his face.

"Okay, team, listen up," said Tazar in his most commanding manner. "I have an announcement I need to make."

Once again Waggit noticed how the team had changed as it gathered around the rock. The dogs were no longer eager to hear what Tazar would say, no longer anticipating a hunt or a game or an expedition to other parts of the park. Now they were apprehensive.

"Olang and I have been talking," Tazar continued,

"and we've come to the decision that the team must no longer have anything to do with Waggit's Upright, Felicia."

A gasp went through the animals, followed by soft murmurs. They were confused; only yesterday Tazar had directed them to camouflage Felicia's tent. Waggit felt all their eyes on him, watching to see what his reaction would be.

"Now here's why I've come to this decision," said Tazar. "Why *we've* come to this decision. Felicia is remarkable, for an Upright. I've never known one like her, and she certainly helped our brother to come back to us. She has ways that none other of her kind have, and she can be very charming. But, and this, my friends, is important—she is still an Upright, and Uprights are the natural enemies of dogs. They cannot be trusted, and we have allowed her to seduce us into trusting her, and we are foolish if we let this continue. Waggit himself knows how treacherous Uprights can be, and yet he still continues to believe there are some good ones in the world. Dogs can't live in peace with an Upright, and neither can Uprights live in peace with us. It isn't natural, and it won't be tolerated. I'll tell you honestly that she had me captivated for a moment,

I won't deny it, but she didn't fool my son here, and I thank him for bringing me back to reality."

There was a stunned silence after Tazar finished talking. Waggit felt the hackles on the back of his neck start to rise, but he knew that getting angry would do him no good, so he tried to calm himself.

"Tazar," he said when he felt composed, "you are the leader of this team, and because of your good leadership we have all survived much adversity. If it weren't for you, I wouldn't be here today; I know that and the rest of the team does too. And it is true that like the rest of us I have suffered much at the hands of Uprights. I have been deceived, abandoned, and betrayed, but you're also right when you say that I believe there must be some good ones among their number. Not all dogs are good, you know that, and I cannot accept that all Uprights are bad. So far Felicia has been generous, kind, and caring. I beg you to reconsider."

Once again silence fell on the team, not a peaceful silence but one that was oppressive and heavy. Tazar looked down at Waggit from his vantage point and addressed him directly.

"Waggit," he said in a quieter but still firm voice, "I have loved you like a son. I have watched you mature.

I have seen you learn to hunt and become wise in the ways of the park. I have witnessed the close bonds grow that tie you in love and affection to all the members of this team. But you have one blind spot, one fatal flaw. You look for good where there is none; you trust and are repaid with deceit. It is your one defect, and it will bring you down, but I will not allow it to bring down the team as well. If you will not do as I say, then you cannot come back to this team. You must live as a loner."

"In that case," Waggit said, his voice trembling slightly, "so be it."

Tazar's eyes widened. This was clearly not the answer he had been expecting.

"Are you telling me that you would take an Upright over the team?" he asked incredulously.

"This is not just *any* Upright," Waggit replied, feeling more confident as he spoke. "This is an Upright who has shown me nothing but kindness, who loves dogs, in fact, is almost a dog herself. Her generosity has not only benefited me but all of us, including you, Tazar. It is wrong of you to test my loyalty to the team by making me betray my loyalty to her. If you wish me to leave the team, then I will, but it will be your decision, not mine."

When he finished speaking his heart was pounding. He had just told his leader, and a dog that he truly admired, that he was wrong. But he stood his ground, looking Tazar straight in the eyes. Murmurs of surprise, and what sounded like agreement, were heard from the other team members.

"No, Waggit, it will be *my* decision."

Everyone whirled around to see Felicia, accompanied by Lug, come out from the trees where she had been standing. She stood tall and dignified as she looked down on Tazar.

"I will not let this happen," she continued. "I will not be the thing that separates Waggit from the team. He loves you all, and he belongs here. You are his life; I am merely passing through. I will leave the park today, and you will see me no more, but before I go think of how I could have served you if I had stayed. I understand your language and that of Uprights, and I can find out what is happening in the park and warn you far quicker than you would otherwise know. I can scavenge food from the Dumpsters at the restaurant without attracting attention." She paused to smile. "I already look like a homeless person anyway, what I believe you call a Skurdie, so nobody would take any notice of me. I have fingers that can remove a burr from a paw. I can do many things, but what I can do most for you is to protect you from my own kind."

Mutterings of "Well, she's got a point," and "It's worth thinking about" were heard from the team, and then Olang spoke for the first time.

"And another thing you can do for us is tell the Ruzelas where we are and help them round us up and take us to the Great Unknown like they did Tashi's team. We've survived very well without your help, and we don't want it now."

Tazar ignored this and turned to address Felicia.

"And why would you do this for us?" he inquired. "Why would you freely offer us these services?"

"Because I like you," she said. "Because I like all of you. I admire your honesty and your loyalty and the way you take care of one another. I wish my species could live the way you live, and some do, but not many. Because it would be fun to spend time with you, and I have nothing better to do for the moment, which doesn't mean that I won't in the future. I am a restless person, and I find it hard to stay anywhere for too long, but for the present I would be happy living here among you."

"And why," said Tazar, "should we trust you to not betray us to the Ruzelas?"

"Look at me," she said. "I'm as much an outsider to them as you are. If they could lock me up in the Great Unknown they would, but they can't. I try not to break too many of their rules, but I don't follow them blindly, either."

Tazar frowned his thoughtful frown.

"I must think about this," he said.

Olang slid up to his father and spoke to him in a whisper that Waggit could just hear.

"What's there to think about, Pa? She's an Upright. You always told me not to trust Uprights, that they're our enemies. They never change. At least, that's what I think, for what it's worth."

"What you think means the world to me," Tazar assured him in a quiet voice. "I have hated Uprights all my life, and with good reason, but maybe this could work for us. To have an Upright on our side, one who can move among them and who understands them, one who speaks their language, well, that would be of real value that we could use. It might be worth taking the risk."

"Well, of course, Father, I will always bow to your judgment," said Olang. "You are infinitely wiser than me. I merely learn the ways of leadership from your example."

"You are a good student, my son," Tazar declared, "and one day you will be a great leader of this team. Your point is well taken, and we will exercise the utmost caution in our dealings with Felicia."

He then turned back to the assembled team and addressed Felicia, who stood in their midst.

"Felicia," he said, "Olang and I have discussed this matter further, and we have decided that we may have judged you too quickly. If you are prepared to do as you say, you can be a great asset for this team. You are welcome to live with us for as long as you like. And Waggit, you are a brother, a team member. Stay with us. You would make a very poor loner."

There were murmurs of approval from the team at Tazar's pronouncement. Felicia looked him directly in the eye and said:

"Thank you, Tazar. I am aware of the high honor you give me, and I will do nothing to betray your trust." She turned her head toward Olang. "But then maybe you cannot betray that which you don't have."

Olang gave her a look of contempt and turned his back on her. Tazar then gave out the assignments of the day to each member of the team, and they began to disperse. As Waggit was walking away Olang came up to him and hissed in his ear:

"You may have won today, Waggit, but that was just a skirmish. The battle is yet to come."

Tazar saw the exchange between the two dogs, and he came up to Waggit after Olang had left.

"What is the problem between you and my son?" he asked. "We don't need discord on the team. It makes everyone join sides, and we become weaker."

"It's not just my problem, Tazar," Waggit replied, dipping into his newfound reservoir of courage. "It's the whole team's problem, including yours."

"And what is this obstacle to harmony that we all share?" Tazar was beginning to sound irritated again.

Waggit took a deep breath. "You remember when you asked me about the team being so down in the mouth?" he asked.

Tazar nodded.

"Well, I didn't tell you then, but I should have." Waggit stopped for a second.

"Tell me what?" asked Tazar.

"It's Olang." Waggit finally got it out. "They are all fearful of Olang. He's a bully and does terrible things, and nobody says a word because he's your son and they don't want to upset you and make you angry, but they're getting angry as well, and he's getting worse."

After this flood of words Tazar sat down and seemed to be deep in thought. He didn't speak for several minutes. Then quietly he asked Waggit, "What kind of terrible things?"

"Well," said Waggit, "he steals food and tells you he made the kill on a hunt when he didn't, and things like that."

"That doesn't sound so terrible," Tazar replied with a smile. "It seems more like a boyish prank or two."

When Waggit thought about it, they did seem like trivial things to complain about. He wished he could remember some of the other incidents that the team told him about, but his mind went blank.

"You know, Waggit," Tazar continued, "the dogs are bound to be jealous of Olang. They know how much I love him, and they know that one day he will be their leader. Oh, I know he gets annoyed when he thinks that they're being lazy or doing stupid things, and he may be a little harsh on them, but he's young.

He's still learning how to be a leader. He's going to be your leader too, and he's going to need your help and your smarts to make this team the best it can be, so let's have no more of this nonsense. Go make up with him."

And with that he brushed warmly against Waggit and walked off, leaving him in the middle of the clearing—speechless.

19

Home Improvement

The dogs resumed their usual occupations. Those who hunted went out in search of prey. Tazar was busy organizing everything, with Olang constantly by his side. As a result of this, Olang actually contributed very little to the daily needs of the team, but strutted around looking bossy. Gruff complained, Alicia preened, and Lowdown spent most of the day lying on rocks warmed by the sun, which he said was the best thing for his old body. One day he was doing just that when Waggit came and lay down beside him.

"Don't tell me your young limbs need warming," Lowdown said.

"No," replied Waggit, "but I've been thinking."

"Oh." Lowdown chortled. "No wonder you need to lie down then!"

"Be serious," said Waggit.

"Pardon me," said Lowdown. "You should've told me this was going to be a serious conversation. I need warning."

"What do you think about the pipe?" Waggit asked, ignoring his last remark.

"I try to think about it as little as possible," Lowdown replied. "It's not great, but we ain't found nothing better, and we scoured the Deepwoods looking for something else."

"It's cramped, and the rain comes in, but the worst thing is there's only one way out. If the Ruzelas were standing at the entrance they'd have us trapped. There's no place to go."

"You're right," agreed Lowdown. "Whenever Olang kept going on about how secure it is I always thought about that. It may be secure but it ain't safe."

"So here's what I've been thinking," continued

Waggit. "We know that for whatever reason the pipe broke in two places, and earth trickled in and blocked the ends. Am I right?"

"So far," said Lowdown.

"But it must've gone somewhere at one time, mustn't it? I mean, Uprights don't go to the bother of burying a pipe for no reason."

"No," agreed Lowdown, "even for them that would be dumb."

"So what I was thinking was," Waggit continued, "why don't we try and dig through the earth at the lower end and see if we can break through to the rest of the pipe? Worst thing is we get more room, and the best would be an escape route."

"You think you could do it?" asked Lowdown. "What would you do with all the dirt you dug out?"

"We'd need to get Felicia to help with that," said Waggit. "It's a job for hands, not paws."

"You're right," agreed Lowdown, "although she could probably persuade the stuff into coming out by itself."

"But what d'you think of it as an idea? Is it worth doing?" asked Waggit.

"I don't see what you've got to lose by trying,"

replied Lowdown, "provided, of course, you don't bring the whole thing down on your heads. You'd better run it past Tazar before you start."

"Of course I'd ask Tazar first," said Waggit. "I just wanted to get your opinion before I go see him."

"Don't forget to talk to him about Olang," Lowdown reminded him.

"I already did," said Waggit miserably.

"And what did he say?" asked Lowdown.

"He told me to make up with Olang."

"Didn't want to hear anything against him, right?"

"Right."

"Oh, well," Lowdown said with a sigh. "At least you tried."

But in his heart Waggit knew he hadn't tried hard enough.

He saw Tazar later on that day and explained his plan in much the same way that he had described it to Lowdown.

"Sounds like an interesting idea," was Tazar's response. "What do you think, Olang?"

"I don't see what's wrong with the pipe as it is now," whined Olang. "I know Waggit doesn't like sleeping there because he's used to more splendid accommodations, but I haven't heard any complaints from the rest of the team, who *do* stay there every night."

"There's nothing wrong with the pipe," Tazar reassured his son. "It's the security aspect of this plan that interests me. It would be easy to be trapped there as it stands now. This is good thinking, Waggit. Well done."

Olang glowered at Waggit when Tazar said this.

When the dogs gathered for the evening meal Tazar cleared his throat and addressed them.

"Listen up," he announced. "Waggit has come up with a plan that might make our living conditions a little better. Tell them about it, Waggit."

Although this wasn't strictly necessary, because Waggit had been enthusiastically telling everyone about it all afternoon, he went through the process again of describing what they would do, how they would do it, and why. When he had finished Tazar said, "I think it's a good plan. We'll start tomorrow. Waggit, Gordo, Cal, and Raz will be diggers, Little One and Little Two will take the dirt away, and Magica and Alona will help Felicia get it out of the pipe and get rid of it. Olang will assist wherever he's needed."

"That'll make a nice change," whispered Lowdown in Waggit's ear.

Waggit had indeed solved the problem of how to dispose of the earth that the diggers removed. Felicia always carried a piece of blue tarpaulin that she used to put under her sleeping bag when the ground was wet. He had figured out that if she tied a piece of string to each corner and shoved the tarpaulin through the entry hole, Little One and Little Two could then take it to where the diggers would be working. The dogs would scoop the earth and rocks onto the tarp, and when there was enough Little One and Little Two would drag it to the entry hole and take the string in their mouths over to Felicia's waiting hands. She would then pull the tarpaulin and the earth up through the hole and dispose of it in a suitable location with the assistance of the two females. Nobody had thought to give Lug a job to do, so he just tagged along with Felicia as usual.

Everyone was up early the following morning, eager to start the project. They were all excited about what might be behind the wall of earth, and each of them claimed to have thought about it before but hadn't said anything to anyone else. Activity always brought out

the best in Tazar, and he marched up and down organizing and giving orders, while Olang spent most of
his time scowling and muttering under his breath that
this was all a waste of time.

There was no room for more than two dogs at the
face of the dig, so Tazar decided that the diggers would
work in shifts. This had the added benefit of reduc-
ing the possibility of injury, because digging too long
could result in broken claws or cut pads.

At first it took Little One and Little Two some time
to get the tarpaulin in position, mostly because the
pipe was so narrow that one of them always ended
up standing on the material as the other tried to tug
it into place. This caused a few growls, but finally it
was ready. The next obstacle was Gordo's enthusiasm combined with his strength. His first attempts
at digging were so energetic that the dirt missed the
tarpaulin altogether and covered Little One and Little
Two from head to paw. When he and Waggit finally
got the hang of getting the dirt on the sheet another
problem occurred. The entry hole was so small that if
there was too much dirt on the tarpaulin it got too big
to pull through. Because only a small quantity of earth
could be brought out each time, the whole process was

slow, but gradually the dirt blocking the pipe became less and less.

Waggit and Gordo were resting above ground while Cal and Raz dug when they heard a howl of excitement from Cal. They rushed into the pipe to find all four dogs who were working down there crowded around the far end. As Waggit ran up to them he could feel a cool breeze of damp, fresh air blowing in his face. The dogs parted to let him through, and there, right in the middle of the earth blocking the pipe, was a small hole through which not only the breeze came, but soft daylight as well. Waggit put one eye to the hole, and he could see that the pipe ran for a considerable distance. At the end he could glimpse filtered sunlight and hear the sound of running water.

"Let me through."

It was the sound of Gordo's booming voice. Everyone stood back and the immense dog went up to the hole, put one muscled front leg through it, and pulled with all his might. Earth came crashing down, but nothing would deter Gordo from his task. All concerns about getting the dirt out were put aside for the time being, and in an incredibly short time the blockage was gone, reduced to piles of soil and rocks that littered the floor.

"Waggit," said Gordo, "it was your idea. You lead the way."

Once again the other dogs stood aside and Waggit walked through into the newly revealed section of the pipe. Moving cautiously along and sniffing the air as he went, he led the others to the end. When they got there they found that it opened up into a rocky pool from which the stream ran. On the opposite side of the pool was another pipe, identical to the one they were standing in, but this one was still working, with a steady flow of water gurgling from it. Waggit looked around and felt relief and pride. His idea had worked. Now this was a home where the team could live forever.

20
Tashi's New Team

The following day was devoted to cleaning up the pipe, and transforming it into a home. Once the dirt and soil were completely removed and all the old newspapers and cardboard taken out, Gordo volunteered to brush the living space out as well as he could using a branch with leaves on it as a broom. It wasn't perfect, given that Gordo filled up the pipe so much that Waggit worried he would get stuck one day, but it was a miracle that it worked as well as it did. It would have worked a little better had it not been for the fact that, walking backward and moving his head from side to side, the big dog found it difficult to judge where he was. He took a step too far and fell into the pond with a resounding splash, which had the added effect of thoroughly washing out the lower part of the pipe.

When the cleaning was considered finished, Tazar, Waggit, and Olang did a tour of inspection. Although the pipe was still narrow, the added length meant that the dogs had more space, especially Lady Alicia, whose long, elegant limbs needed a lot of room, and who didn't like other dogs too close to her. Tazar looked around approvingly.

"You did the team a good service thinking of this, Waggit," he said. "I don't know why I didn't come up with the idea myself."

"Actually, Father, the thought occurred to me also, when I first found the pipe," Olang claimed, "but what I worried about was that if there was another opening it would mean there would be two places we have to guard. Anywhere we can get out, our enemies can get in."

"And you were right to be concerned about that," Tazar congratulated him. "That's the kind of strategic planning a leader has to do. As it turns out, though, because the pipe opens up into a pool it's much less likely that anyone would attack from that end. It's too deep for any dog to easily make it from the water into the pipe. We will never forget," he added, "that it was you who found the pipe in the first place."

Waggit didn't think this was the time to bring up the fact that Olang hadn't found it but had just taken credit for its discovery. When they had completed their inspection and deemed the new, bigger space suitable for canine habitation, they came out and told the team to go and find new bedding, each dog being responsible for his or her own sleeping arrangements. They all agreed that Lowdown would continue to sleep wherever it was that he spent the night—Waggit was still the only team member who knew the location. Lug would stay with Felicia, but the rest of the team would be together in their improved quarters. Out of deference to his son's comments Tazar reorganized the sentry duty, placing one dog at each end of the pipe.

Waggit had decided that he should stop sleeping in Lowdown's tree trunk and stay in the pipe. He had chosen a place near the pond end, and had furnished it with a flattened cardboard box and a layer of newspaper, all topped off with some fern leaves. He tested it out that afternoon, and it seemed comfortable, with a gentle breeze ruffling the sheets of paper. It might not be such a great spot in the winter, but for now it was perfect.

When darkness fell, however, one of its disadvantages became apparent. The sky was moonless, and although it never got totally dark in the park because of the city's glow, this was about as deep a night as ever happened. The spot where Waggit had placed his bed was pitch-black. As a result of this, his attempt to get to it was accompanied by a series of growls and squeaks as he trod on various parts of several dogs. Once finally there he turned around a couple of times to get the fern leaves just the way he wanted them and lay down with a sigh of satisfaction. He had no sooner settled when he heard Tazar's voice at the entrance.

"Waggit, you down there?"

"Yes, Tazar," Waggit answered. "I'm in bed."

"Get up here," said Tazar. "I need to talk to you."

Waggit sighed again, this time not in satisfaction, and walked back the way he had come. The return journey was somewhat easier because his eyes had become accustomed to the dark, but there were still a couple of complaints. One of them, predictably, was from Gruff, who said he thought it was about time that the younger generation showed some respect for the limbs of their elders, and that if Waggit wanted to spend the entire night marching up and down he should go on sentry duty.

Ignoring this, Waggit climbed out of the pipe and into the night where Tazar was waiting for him. The black dog nodded and they both walked to a nearby rock that had weathered into a shallow cave. They sat down, their backs to the rock, facing out.

"I hate these black nights," said Tazar. "You only get bad news on nights like this."

"And did you?" asked Waggit.

"Did I what?" said Tazar, whose mind seemed to be on something else.

"Get bad news?" Waggit repeated.

"Maybe," replied Tazar. "It depends on if it's true or not. I was talking to a loner who said she had heard Tashi's put together another team, and this one makes the first lot look like petulants."

One of Tazar's great skills was in using the stray dogs who lived by themselves as a source of news. This was not as easy as it sounds, because most of them were too shy or fearful to talk to another dog and would scuttle away as soon as you approached them. If you could get them to talk, what they told you was usually true, because they had no need to lie, exaggerate, or impress you. Because of this the news the loner had given Tazar was not good. Tashi's followers had been a fearsome group, tough and aggressive, who would bite you in the throat without thinking twice about it, but most of them had been captured in a raid by the park rangers and taken to the pound. Only Tashi and his evil lieutenant, Wilbur, had escaped, much to the scorn of Tazar, who thought that a leader should stick with his dogs to the end.

"Where do you think he got his team?" Waggit inquired.

"I have no idea," said Tazar. "A lot of miscreants turn up in the park. I mean, if you were an Upright living with a dog like Tashi, you'd more than likely get rid of him too."

While this was probably true, it made Waggit uncomfortable to think that there was any justifiable reason for abandoning a dog, even Tashi.

"What shall we do about it?" he asked Tazar.

"We need to get more information," the leader said. "I asked this loner to see what else she could find out, like how many there are and where their camp is, that sort of thing."

Just then Olang appeared from out of the darkness.

"Ah, there you are, Father," he said. "Having a little chat with Waggit?"

"I was telling him about the situation with Tashi," explained Tazar.

"The same situation we discussed several hours ago?" asked Olang, insinuating that Waggit was getting old news.

"The same," said Tazar. "We've got to devise a plan to handle these new circumstances."

"Why don't I ask Felicia to see what she can find out from the Ruzelas?" Waggit suggested.

"But can we trust her to tell us the truth?" Olang said with a sneer.

"I don't see that we have any choice," said Tazar. "It's not like we can talk to the Ruzelas ourselves, and the more you know about a situation the easier it is to handle." He paused and sighed. "I tell you, these black nights are when evil stalks a dog."

The following morning after breakfast Waggit took Felicia to one side and explained the situation to her.

"Well of course I'll help," she said, "but I think I'll go by myself. Better to leave Alona and Lug here."

"Whatever you say," agreed Waggit.

Alona and Lug went everywhere with Felicia nowadays. They had almost become a team within the team, and it was an indication to Waggit how seriously concerned Felicia was about the state of affairs that she would leave them behind. He also realized how much a part of the team she had become. The Tazarians didn't treat her any differently than they would treat another dog, and even Tazar himself occasionally asked her advice. No sooner had Felicia left on her mission, however, than Olang, seeing Lug without his companion, crept up behind him. When he was close to the pit bull he let out his loudest, most ferocious bark, which caused Lug to jump in the air and come crashing down. As he was lying quivering on the ground, Olang came over to him and bared his teeth.

"Oh, Lug," he sneered. "Did I scare you? I'm so sorry! Please don't tell your protector, the Upright, because I would hate to upset her. She's so important to the team—for the time being at least."

Waggit, seeing what was happening, ran over and pushed Olang aside.

"Let him be, Olang," he growled.

"Why, I quite forgot," Olang taunted Lug, "that of course you have two bodyguards, the Upright and the saintly Waggit. What a lucky little worm you are!"

Waggit ignored him and stood over Lug until he could get back on his feet.

"Take no notice, Lug," he said. "Let's you and I go for a walk."

And the two of them left Olang snickering to himself.

As they walked along Waggit looked at the other dog. It was strange that he was so fainthearted. He was strong and muscular and had a fearsome appearance on the outside. But inside—well, Waggit had seen rabbits with more courage. He stopped and turned to Lug.

"Why are you so scared of everything?" Waggit asked. "What happened to you to make you so fearful?"

"I'm scared of pain," replied Lug.

"Well, none of us like it," said Waggit, "but you're terrified of it."

"You know I told you about the Upright at the bar who used to feed me?" Lug continued. "For an Upright he was a decent enough sort of guy. He didn't have to give me food and water, but he did. Well, early one day, when he was by himself, two men came into the bar. One was holding a metal tube with a handle that he pointed at the man, and it scared him. These two took lots of bottles from behind the bar, and all that stuff Felicia calls money from a drawer in the counter. I had no idea what was happening, so I stayed under a table where they couldn't see me."

"What happened next?" asked Waggit.

"The two men ran off with all the stuff," replied Lug, "and then the Upright from the bar spotted me under the table and gave me the most awful kick. I ran out into the open, which was the worst thing I could do, because he came after me with one of the cloths they used to wipe the bar with. It was wet, and when he hit me it stung terribly. He kept on hitting me and hitting me, and when the towel started to dry out he wet it again so that it hurt more. He beat me for so long I thought I was going to die."

"Why didn't you run away?"

"Where could I go?" cried Lug. "It was a small town, and no one else was going to feed me, that I was sure of. I did leave for a couple of days, but in the end I had to come back."

"Did he beat you again?"

"No. I think the reason he did it then was because he was scared and it was the only way he could get rid of the fear. So, no, he didn't beat me again, but every time he wanted to shoo me out of the bar he would get the wet cloth and show it to me and it would make me panic. I think he thought it was funny."

"I'm sorry that happened to you." Waggit tried to console him. "It's the same as me being scared of being abandoned. It may never happen again, but I can't forget what it felt like."

"That's why I like Felicia," said Lug. "When I'm with her the scare seems to go away. I'm always happy when I'm with her."

They didn't see any more of Felicia until late that afternoon. Most of the dogs were sitting around nervously talking about Tashi. Only Olang was absent, but since he often disappeared for hours at a time, this wasn't unusual. When Felicia returned she had a grim look on her face. The dogs' ears pricked up as she approached, and they gathered around to hear what she had to say. Tazar greeted her.

"Okay," he said, "let me guess—you bring us bad news."

"I wish it was otherwise," replied Felicia, "but I'm afraid the situation is grave. There have been three dog attacks in the park that are worrying the Ruzelas—two runners and one cyclist, and one of the runners was badly bitten on her leg."

The team remained silent, for they all knew what this meant—every dog not in the company of a human would now be at risk. The park rangers wouldn't bother to identify which of them had participated in the attacks; from now on any animals by themselves would be considered guilty.

"It gets worse, I'm afraid," Felicia continued. "The attack on the cyclist was within a short distance of here."

"What's a cyclist?" asked Gordo.

"Someone on a bike," explained Felicia. The blank stares she received meant she had to be more descriptive. "You know, like a car, only with two wheels instead of four."

"Oh," said Cal. "You mean a half-roller."

"Why didn't she say so if that's what she meant?" said Gruff crossly.

"Do they know what kind of dogs were involved in the attacks?" asked Tazar.

"They only know about the dogs that went after the runners. They were led by one that looked like . . ." Felicia paused. "Well, very much like Lug, actually."

"Me," squealed Lug. "Me! I don't attack! I don't even lead."

"I didn't say it was you," said Felicia patiently. "I just said the dog looked like you."

"It wasn't you, Lug," said Tazar. "It was Tashi. You look a whole lot like Tashi. In fact the first time I saw you I thought you must be some kind of relative of his."

"I know I look like Tashi!" exclaimed Lug. "I've been told that before. But we're not relatives."

"Well," said Tazar, "I have some news too, only it's a bit better than Felicia's. I spoke to the loner again today, and she told me that Tashi does have a new team, and a pretty sad one at that. First of all it's small, fewer than the claws on one paw, and they aren't ferocious at all. It's made up of the most broken-down misfits you ever saw in your life. Oh, and another thing, Tashi makes them all let him bite off the tip of one of their ears as a sign of loyalty to him."

"Yeeeach," screeched Alicia, "that's disgusting. I

mean, I'm as loyal as the next dog, but ain't no one gonna take a piece out of my ear."

"Did the loner know where they live?" asked Waggit.

"Not exactly," said Tazar. "She knew they were still on the Goldenside, and she thought nearer to the Deepwoods, but she'd never seen their camp herself."

"Why, then, would they attack Uprights in this part of the park?" asked Magica.

"That's easy," said Tazar. "Somebody's told them this is our new realm, and they're trying to get the Ruzelas up this way so we'll either get captured or have to move. What they didn't think of, because Tashi's too dumb, is that any attack on an Upright is bad news for all the free dogs, not just us."

Felicia had a look of deep concern on her face.

"How will you handle this?" she asked Tazar.

"We'll have to lie low for a few days. The Ruzelas will soon lose interest, providing there are no more attacks. As for Tashi," he said in a matter-of-fact tone, "we're going to have to tussle. I should've done it many risings ago, but it never happened. Remember, Waggit, when we set it up and there was nobody home, because they'd all been captured?"

Waggit nodded.

"Well, this time," said Tazar, "he won't slip away. This time it'll be a fight to the death."

21
Treachery at Silver Tree Bend

Tazar's prediction that all would be well if there were no more attacks and they laid low proved to be correct. In fact where the Tazarians lived there was no increase in human activity whatsoever. Felicia brought back daily reports from the section of the park south of the Deepwoods, which Waggit realized no longer played a part in their lives. It was almost as if a pact had been made whereby the Ruzelas stayed in their area and the dogs never left the safety of the woods. The only contact they had with that world was through Felicia.

"They're doing sweeps along the Goldenside, but as I understand it not far enough up to get Tashi," she reported one afternoon. "At least nobody's been captured yet."

"That makes sense," Tazar remarked, "because that's where the worst attack was. Any idea if they're planning to come to our neck of the woods?"

"None that I've heard," Felicia replied.

"They'll never come up this way," sneered Olang. "They're too scared. One thing about attacking Uprights, it certainly keeps them away."

"Attacking Uprights is dumb," said Tazar. "It always was dumb and it always will be dumb."

"But, Pa," whined Olang, "you taught us that Uprights are our enemy, and if that's true then we have to fight them."

"No!" growled Tazar sharply. "We do not. I also taught you never to fight unless you've got at least a chance of winning—with Uprights that will never happen. If anyone on this team is caught attacking Uprights they will be banished immediately, whoever they are. If you want to fight, fight Tashi."

"Sounds like a coward's way out to me," Olang muttered under his breath.

"What was that?" snarled Tazar.

"Nothing, Father. Nothing."

Waggit was shocked by this exchange. He had never heard Tazar speak to his son in such a stern manner. From the stunned silence that followed he assumed that none of the other team members had either. After the gathering broke up, Waggit and Lowdown went back to Lowdown's tree. The old dog liked to rest before the evening meal, and often he and Waggit would spend the time talking about this and that. The first topic that afternoon was Tazar scolding Olang.

"I've never heard him be that sharp with Olang before," Waggit remarked. "I've never heard him give Olang anything but praise."

"Lately I've noticed a slight change in his attitude toward his son," said Lowdown. "Sometimes—not often—he gets irritated with him. It's probably your fault, you know."

"My fault?" exclaimed Waggit. "How can it possibly be my fault?"

"You're right," agreed Lowdown. "Fault's the wrong word. But you're the reason he's looking at Olang in a different light. Now that you're back Tazar's got someone to compare him to, and next to you he don't look too good."

"You really think so?" Waggit was incredulous.

"I really do," said Lowdown, "and I'll tell you something else. Olang may not be the sharpest tooth in the mouth, but he knows it too, and don't think he ain't gonna try and get back at you for it. He knows you're a threat to him, not just for his father's affections, but also for the leadership of the team."

"The leadership?" Waggit spluttered. "I'm not going to be the leader. Whatever put that in your head?"

"You're a natural leader," Lowdown assured him. "I know it, the team knows it, and Olang knows it too."

Waggit was dumbfounded.

"I just hope for once in your life you're wrong, Lowdown," he said.

"It wouldn't be the first time." The old dog chuckled. "But in this case I don't think so."

Over the next few days Olang behaved as Lowdown predicted. Everything came to a head one afternoon when, once again, Felicia was the bearer of bad news.

"I'm sorry to have to tell you, but there's been another attack in this area," she told the assembled team.

"Another half-roller?" asked Tazar.

"Indeed," she confirmed.

"And do they have a description of the dog who did it?" asked Olang.

"Well—yes—actually I believe they do," said Felicia uncomfortably.

"Will you share it with us?" persisted Olang.

"I believe, from what I've heard, that the dog— well, it seems that the dog involved in the attack was white," Felicia went on, as if every word she uttered gave her pain.

"How interesting," said Olang as he turned toward Waggit.

The other dogs followed his lead until all eyes were staring in disbelief at the white dog. Tazar stood to his full imposing height and walked over to Waggit.

"Tell me it's not true," he said quietly, and with sadness in his voice.

"It's not true," Waggit replied calmly, and with as much composure as possible.

"Well," Olang said with a sigh, "I don't see any other white dogs around here, do you?"

Indeed nobody knew of another white dog or could ever remember there being one among the free dogs. There were plenty of pets with that coloring, but it was unlikely that they would be attacking cyclists in the Deepwoods.

"You are somewhat distinctive," said Tazar. "If it wasn't you, then who was it?"

"I don't know, but ask yourself this, Tazar. Why would I attack Uprights?" said Waggit. "You think I have too soft a spot for them anyway."

"Maybe," Olang speculated, "in some twisted way Waggit thought he was proving his loyalty to the team, that he could be trusted, that he wasn't a spy for the Uprights. He may have done it even though, Father, you yourself said any dog caught attacking an Upright would be exiled."

Waggit began to panic.

"It's not true, it really isn't. I didn't do anything. Felicia, why did you tell them that? Why couldn't you have kept it to yourself?"

"Waggit, the team would have found out anyway," she said with regret in her voice. Waggit looked wildly around at the staring eyes. He knew that going to pieces wouldn't help him, but he couldn't control his fear and anger.

"It wasn't me, I swear it. Please believe me, I didn't do it. I didn't do it."

He stopped, his body shaking with terror. He knew that if Tazar didn't believe that he was innocent the black dog had the power to send him away from his friends, from his home, from everything for which he had journeyed back to the park. However much the other dogs liked him, none of them would disobey the leader. That was the law by which they lived.

"I didn't do it," he cried, "and you can't prove that I did."

"No," said Tazar. "You're right; we cannot prove it. But if you are innocent you have nothing to be scared of, and yet you are scared. What, then, is making you so fearful?"

"Because I know you don't believe me," Waggit replied, "and because I know that Olang is trying . . ."

He got no further, but was interrupted by a roar from Tazar.

"Enough about Olang," he bellowed. "Everything bad that happens cannot be blamed on Olang, and I will not tolerate you sowing the seeds of dissension among us. I am not only beginning to doubt your honesty but your motives as well. Olang *will* be the leader of this team, and if you cannot live with that you cannot live with us. Give me one good reason why I should not banish you now."

A gasp of shock ran through the dogs, and silence fell upon the scene. Then, from the edge of the woods, came a soft but clear voice.

"Tazar, I think I can give you that reason." It was Alona, and behind her stood one of her loner friends, keeping in the shadows, nervous and apprehensive.

"Come forward, Alona," said Tazar. "Tell us your reason."

"This is one of the loners what lives at the far end of the Deepwoods." She indicated the animal accompanying her. He looked backward and forward at everyone, the whites of his eyes showing and his ears flat to his head.

"I brought him here because he told me something that at first I didn't understand, but it makes perfect sense now."

"And that is?" asked Tazar.

"He witnessed the attack on the Upright, the one on the half-roller." A murmur passed through the team.

"According to him," Alona continued, "it *was* a white dog what done the attack—but it weren't Waggit."

"Then who?" asked Tazar.

"One of Tashi's new team. He got to the park only

a few risings ago. He's an evil piece of work by all accounts, and he's pure white," she replied.

"Are you sure of this?" Tazar asked the loner.

"Oh yes, sir, absolutely sure, your honor," he replied, quivering the whole time.

"But that's not the most interesting part," continued Alona. "The bit what I find strange is that just before the attack he saw another dog urging the white dog on."

"Do you know the other dog?" asked Tazar.

"Yes, your highness, I'm afraid I do," the loner answered.

"Then tell us who it was," demanded Tazar.

"It was your son, sir. It was Olang."

There was a bellow from Olang, who sprang forward, his fangs bared, causing Alona to scuttle back into the shadows next to her informant.

"That's a lie," snarled Olang. "That's a dirty, stinking lie!"

"If I find out that it's true," warned Tazar, "I will banish you, even though you are my flesh and blood. If you've been conspiring with Tashi or one of his dogs, you cannot be trusted to live among us."

"I just told you it's not true," insisted Olang. "Why would you believe a loner over me?"

"In all the years I've been in this park," replied his father, "I have never known a loner to lie. They have no need to. They gain nothing from untruths."

"Well, you just met the first one that lies," growled Olang, his eyes narrowed and foam forming at the corners of his mouth. "Go to Silver Tree Bend and see if you can find one paw mark that looks like mine, just one. I challenge you."

Tazar looked at his son, and the dogs could see the hurt in his eyes.

"Olang, if you weren't there, how do you know the attack took place at Silver Tree Bend?"

"She said that's where it was." Olang nodded toward Felicia. "That Upright hag said so."

"No, Olang," said Felicia. "I never mentioned it."

"Well, it must've been that loner deadbeat you took in, that Alona." For the first time Olang was beginning to look scared rather than outraged.

"Nobody but you mentioned Silver Tree Bend," said Tazar. "Nobody but you knew."

Olang looked around at the dogs who surrounded him. His aggressive stance changed as he saw their hostility toward him, and he tried to act unconcerned.

"Okay, so maybe I did have a little chat with Tashi.

Is that a crime?" he asked. "He's not such a bad fellow. I think if you got to know him better, Pa, you'd find you have many things in common."

"I have known Tashi longer than you've been alive," growled Tazar, "and I know that he's pure evil and that he turns everything he touches and everyone he knows into evil."

"Well, one thing you don't have in common is that, evil or not, he's prepared to take the fight to the Uprights. He knows you have to fight for what's rightfully yours. *He's* not afraid of them."

Tazar ignored the implications of this last remark.

"What worries me most," he said with a sigh, "is not that you have been consorting with our bitter enemy, but that you have tried to turn us from your brother here with your scheming, and you would have caused me to make a terrible mistake had it not been for sister Alona."

"You can't blame me for trying to get rid of him." Olang scowled. "Ever since he came back it's been Waggit this and Waggit that. Waggit's such a good hunter. Waggit has such good ideas. Waggit's a natural leader. I'm sick of hearing about Waggit. I'm your son, Pa, your own kin, and yet you seem to care more about him than me. I'm going to be leader of this team, not him. You promised me."

"Not only will you not be leader of this team," said Tazar solemnly, "you will not even be a member of it. From now on I banish you from our realm. You will live the life of a loner until you see the error of your ways. If you truly repent, then we will consider having you back, but that will be many risings from now."

"You cannot banish me," roared Olang. "It is I that banish you and your pathetic group of losers. From now on you have no son, unless of course," he sneered, "you adopt the saintly Waggit."

He glared at his father with anger in his eyes, turned his back on him, and walked away. As he got to the others he snarled at them with contempt. They parted to let him through and he disappeared into the woods.

22
Triumph and Tragedy

Olang's departure and the resurgence of Tashi with his new team were the main topics of discussion among the Tazarians in the days that followed. If Tazar was upset by his son's banishment he didn't show it.

"He must be feeling terrible about exiling Olang," Waggit said to Lowdown during one of their afternoon conversations, "but he just carries on like nothing happened."

"Don't be fooled by that," Lowdown assured him. "Tazar always said being a leader comes before everything else. That don't mean he ain't hurtin' though."

Tazar was now depending more and more on Waggit, almost as if he had taken to heart Olang's sarcastic suggestion that he adopt the white dog. He didn't have a lot of time to fret about his wayward boy, because much of his attention was taken up by worrying about the reemergence of Tashi.

"I heard that one of the kitchen workers at the restaurant was badly bitten trying to shoo away some Tashinis from the Dumpsters," Felicia reported one day. "This is the third attack in as many weeks, and everyone is saying that something has to be done about the wild dogs."

"The reason that creature is dangerous," said Tazar, referring to Tashi, "is because he's so stupid. He's all muscle and no mind, and he's making life for the rest of us more precarious than it needs to be."

"What can we do?" asked Waggit.

"The first thing we've got to do is find out the location of his camp," replied Tazar. "We can't make plans until we know where he is."

And so the team spent a lot of time trying to track down Tashi's hideout, but as so often happens, in the end they found it by accident. Waggit, Cal, Raz, and Magica were hunting one morning. Their prey was a rabbit, but it was young and fast, so they chased it longer and farther than they would have normally. The pursuit even took them across the road that went around the inside of the park. Fortunately it was closed to traffic at the time, although Magica nearly collided with a cyclist.

Coming down a hill where the Deepwoods gave way to more open ground, Waggit stopped dead in his tracks so suddenly that the others who were following nearly crashed into him, while the rabbit fled into the undergrowth.

"Whassup?" asked Cal.

"Quietly," said Waggit. "Look down there."

The other three dogs followed Waggit's gaze, and there, next to a large clump of bushes, were Tashi and Wilbur, their heads together, talking to each other intently. They were unaware that they were being watched when, out of the bushes, came a third dog, a sad-looking specimen, malnourished, with a scruffy coat and half of his left ear missing. Tashi snarled at him, and he cowered away in fear and lay on the ground looking up at his leader. As he did so he caught sight of the spies on the hill out of the corner of his eye and alerted Tashi, who whirled around and started to walk menacingly toward them.

"Let's go," said Waggit. "This is neither the time nor the place."

The four of them fled back the way they came. When they arrived at the pipe they had to rest for a while to regain their breath before they could tell Tazar what had happened. They finally stopped panting enough to be able to describe Tashi's camp and its location.

"Still living in bushes, huh?" said Tazar. "That's pathetic. You'd think after what happened he would've learned his lesson."

It was true that Tashi's old camp had also been in the bushes. These provided adequate shelter during the summer, when the canopy of leaves kept out most of the weather, but their biggest disadvantage was that they were difficult to defend. Both the tunnel and now the pipe, after its recent renovations, had escape routes of which a potential attacker would be unaware until it was too late.

"What're you gonna do, boss?" asked Lowdown, who had been listening to the hunters tell their tale.

"He has to go," Tazar answered, "and this time he's got to go for good."

"One on one," said Lowdown, "or team against team?"

"One on one," replied Tazar, "but I want the team with me."

"When d'you want to do it?" asked Waggit.

"There's no time like the present," said Tazar, "and we know he's home."

He organized the team, ordering Lowdown, Gruff, and Alicia to remain and look after the pipe. Waggit went to the willow tree to find Felicia, to warn her about what was happening and tell her to stay away. This was going to be strictly for dogs. When he got there Lug was all by himself.

"Where's Felicia?" he asked Lug.

"Dunno," Lug replied. "She went off a while ago and told me to stay here."

"Well," said Waggit, "it's for the best; she'd be upset by the tussle."

"By the what?" said Lug nervously.

"The tussle," said Waggit. "We're going to tussle with Tashi."

"When you say we . . ." Lug's voice trailed off.

"Don't worry," said Waggit, "not you, and not me, either. Tazar's taking on Tashi, and we have to be there to back him up. Come on."

With the look on his face of someone who really did not want to be doing what he was doing, Lug reluctantly followed Waggit back to the pipe. When they got there the rest of the team was ready to set out. They did so silently but determinedly, moving at a steady pace toward the spot where Waggit and the others knew Tashi's camp to be. Instead of coming down the hill that the hunters had taken, they went by an alternate route that brought them onto the flat open ground in front of the bushes that were the rival team's home. Tazar moved ahead of the others and stood by himself.

"Tashi," he shouted in his deepest, most resonant voice, "get your miserable, petulant body out here."

"Well, well, well, visitors. How nice. I thought we might be having visitors."

It was Tashi's voice all right, but it was not coming from the bushes. Tazar and the team whirled around to see Tashi and a bedraggled group of dogs, including one very white one, standing on a rock halfway up the hill from which the hunters had first seen him.

"Okay, Tashi," said Tazar, "your time's up. You and me, now."

"Well, I don't know about that," sneered Tashi. "Maybe before I decide I should consult with my newest recruit."

He moved to one side to reveal Olang standing behind him with a smirk on his face and half of his left ear missing. Upon seeing his son Tazar froze, and at the same time Tashi launched himself off the rock with a snarl. He landed in front of the still paralyzed Tazar and was just about to pounce when Waggit jumped into the fray.

He leapt at Tashi, his teeth bared, and made contact with his hard, muscled shoulder. Tashi howled in pain, spun around, and threw his full weight at him. Waggit's slender body was made for speed, not for fighting, and it was immediately apparent that he was hopelessly outclassed by the tough, strong dog. Tashi soon had him on his back and Waggit could hear his opponent's teeth snapping together as he tried to go for his throat. He knew that if those powerful jaws ever got around his neck he would be dead, and he desperately clawed at Tashi's body in a futile attempt to get him off.

He suddenly heard a thump, and Tashi's body was lifted clean off the ground. To Waggit's complete amazement he rolled over to see Lug furiously fighting with their enemy. Tazar, who seemed to have recovered from his shock, now stood with an astonished look on his face as he watched the most timid dog anyone had ever known attacking the toughest.

Waggit, Tazar, and the other members of the team tried to intervene in the intense combat, but the action was so fearsome and violent that nobody could get close, nor would they have been able to separate the two. They would have been just as likely to bite Lug as Tashi, as the two of them rolled over and over, first one on top and then the other. Because both dogs looked so similar it was often hard to tell them apart. As the fight continued both teams gathered around, their enmity momentarily forgotten, mesmerized by the action.

The Tazarians gasped when they thought they saw Tashi's teeth sink into Lug's flesh, and cheered Lug on when it appeared he had Tashi on the ground. Then, as quickly as it had started, it ended. Lug moved away from Tashi and sat, panting hard, covered in Tashi's blood. Tashi lay prostrate on the ground, blood pouring from his many wounds. He looked up at Tazar with loathing in his eyes.

"My dying curse on you, Tazar. May it follow you forever."

These were his last words as his malevolent eyes closed and he lay still. The Tazarians gathered around Lug, telling him how brave he was, what a good fighter, and how they all owed him a big debt. Waggit could see how proud the victorious dog was, and he realized that Lug was now as much a part of the team as he was himself. Then over all the congratulations and expressions of admiration came the voice of Tazar.

"So, Olang," he cried, "is this your final betrayal?"

"No, Father, you're the one who betrayed me," replied Olang, "with all your 'Oh, the team's so great,' and 'Oh, Lowdown's so wise,' and 'Oh, Waggit's just like a son.' Well, what about me? What about my feelings? What about your real son? I didn't betray you. It was you who forced me to find another father, and now you've taken *him* away as well."

Tazar stood there, gazing at his son, a pitiful look on his face. At that moment the entire team could see the intense grief that he had been covering up.

"Olang, come back home." Tazar broke down. "I love the team, but I love you more. Come home and let's forgive each other."

"You may forgive me, but I'll never forgive you. You may have killed one enemy, but another has sprung up in his place. I will not rest until I avenge Tashi's death."

He turned, cast one last hateful look over his shoulder, and with Wilbur and the assortment of pathetic creatures that had been Tashi's team by his side, he disappeared once again into the woods.

The Tazarians stood there awkwardly, not quite knowing what to do next, when suddenly they heard a thump behind them. They all turned to see Lug lying on the ground, a large crimson pool spreading beneath his body. Waggit ran over to him, and then he saw the terrible wound in the dog's neck. They had all assumed he was covered in Tashi's blood, but, in fact, most of it was his own. Waggit started to lick Lug all over his face, and the fallen animal looked up at him with a proud expression.

"I *was* brave, wasn't I, Waggit?" he asked faintly.

"You were very, very brave," said Waggit. "You saved my life."

"That's only fair," replied Lug. "You saved mine a couple of times."

"Be still," said Waggit. "Rest easy."

There was silence as Lug breathed shallowly.

"It feels good to be brave, doesn't it, Waggit?" he whispered.

"Yes," agreed Waggit, "it does."

"I'm not going to be scared anymore. I'm going to be brave for the rest of my life."

Waggit lay down by Lug's side, still licking his face, warming the injured dog with his body. Lug looked up at him, smiled peacefully, and then was no more.

23
Chance Meeting

People think that dogs can't cry. They can. It's just that their tears run down their noses instead of coming out of their eyes. That day, and for several days to come, there were many sniffly noses on the team. Everyone agreed that Lug would have made a fine Tazarian had he lived, and that his strength and newfound courage would have been invaluable to the team. They also agreed that they should have been kinder to him, should have seen his good qualities instead of dismissing him for his timidity. Nobody felt this more than

Waggit. Lug was dead, killed while saving Waggit's life. It was a weight that he felt he would carry for as long as he lived.

The scene that confronted them when they returned to the pipe didn't help either. They left Gordo guarding Lug's body while they went back to tell Felicia what had happened, only to find her beaming with pleasure. In front of her was another of the celebratory feasts that she occasionally put together when she felt their spirits needed lifting or when they had done something particularly noteworthy.

"Why, there you all are," she said as she fussed around, arranging the food in a pile for each team member. "I thought we would have a little meal together to celebrate Waggit, Lug, and me being in the park for three months, which, as you know, is a quarter of a year."

She glanced up from what she was doing and saw for the first time the long faces and sad body language of the animals in front of her.

"Something terrible has happened, hasn't it?" she asked.

They told her the whole story, and by the time they finished tears were rolling down her cheeks.

"Oh my," she said, "that poor, brave boy. Such courage, such heroism. What a tragedy."

None of which made them feel any better.

When Felicia had stopped crying they went back to where Gordo was guarding Lug's body. She bent down, gently picked him up, and holding him closely to her chest she carried him back to the big willow tree where she and Lug had spent his last night. She lay him down on the earth near the tree, and the team gathered around silently in a circle. The silence lasted until Tazar went over to the body and spoke to it.

"Brother Lug, you have slain our enemy. Because of your sacrifice all the creatures who live in the park are safer. You also saved the life of our dear brother Waggit. Because of your love for him you found the courage you didn't know you had. May all of us in this team live bravely through the love we feel for each other, and may we find the strength through the team that we couldn't find by ourselves."

Once more there was silence as each of the dogs looked down at Lug. It was broken by Alicia, who spoke in a remarkably subdued voice.

"You know, he may not have been a purebred, but he was a good guy."

This was about the highest praise she could have given, and nobody felt they needed to add more.

"We must bury him," said Tazar, "before the Ruzelas come and throw him away like trash."

And so they each took turns to dig a hole just downstream from the willow tree. Everyone wanted to do his or her part toward the excavation. Even Lowdown managed a few scoops of earth with his arthritic legs. Soon there was a deep hole that was to be Lug's final home. Felicia laid his body in it along with two rawhide chews. "Just in case," she said, without saying in case of what. The team then pushed the earth back, and as the dirt began to pile up on his remains they worked quicker, fearful that their hearts would break before the task was finished. When the hole was filled in Felicia dragged some large rocks over to cover it up, and at the end of one of the rocks she made a little pile of stones standing on top of each other to form a small tower so they would always know where he was and always remember him.

Later on, as that terrible day drew to a close, Waggit lay in the spot where Lug used to sleep in Felicia's tent.

"I should have been nicer to him," he said.

"He irritated you," she replied. "You couldn't help feeling it any more than he could help doing it. It was just the way it was. And don't forget, *you* saved *his* life *twice*! If you hadn't gone after those men behind the bar I don't think that there's any doubt they would have killed him, and you risked your own life and possible capture to give me enough time to get him out of the Dumpster."

"I suppose so," said Waggit, although he didn't sound convinced.

"You were very brave then. Why do you think Lug was so in awe of you? It was because he saw in you the courage that he didn't think he had," said Felicia. "He knew that you found him annoying, but he also knew that he could rely on you, and that you would take care of him."

Waggit sighed and lay against Felicia. The warmth of her body was consoling, just as the warmth of Lowdown's, Gordo's, or any of the other team members was comforting. In fact, he thought, he didn't consider her human at all, but more like a very large, two-legged dog, and he was pretty sure that the rest of the team felt the same way. Tonight he would sleep in the tent, but tomorrow he would return to his brothers and sisters in the pipe. His place was with them and he knew it, but tonight he would stay with his tall friend and take solace from her compassion.

Each member of the team reacted to the tragedy in a different way in the days that followed. Alona went back to being the solitary dog she had been before she joined the team and was rarely seen at all; Gordo ate even more when food was available and obsessively chewed sticks when it wasn't; Tazar covered up his pain by relentlessly organizing everything and everyone; Magica mothered Little One and Little Two even though both dogs were now well beyond the age and size where mothering was needed; Alicia groomed herself so much that the other dogs were worried she would actually lick off parts of her coat and leave bald spots.

It wasn't just grief that the team had to face, but fear as well. Even though Tazar's speech had moved them all, it wasn't entirely accurate. If Olang led Tashi's old team the way the pit bull himself had, and if the attacks on humans continued, as it seemed Olang was threatening, then the Tazarians were no safer than they had been before Tashi's death. Furthermore, Olang, unlike Tashi, knew exactly where the pipe was and where the sentries were posted. It was a situation that made everybody very nervous.

Waggit divided his time between Lowdown and Felicia. Each of them gave him comfort in their own ways. Lowdown always had the ability to look at life's events, both good and bad, philosophically, neither exaggerating nor denying their importance, but putting them into a perspective that Waggit found reassuring. Felicia provided him with a connection to Lug. Waggit would go for long walks with her and talk about their lost companion, which would then lead to other subjects, such as the nature of courage, and loyalty, and any number of things that the young dog was thinking about for the first time.

It was on one such occasion that the two friends were walking along the Risingside. It was one of those early autumn days that are warm and almost springlike. Waggit was feeling better than he had in several days and trotted along beside Felicia, who was holding on to the leash she always attached when a dog was accompanying her to the more populated areas of the park. They had been talking of this and that, nothing of great importance, when she suddenly felt the leash go tight. She turned to look at Waggit, who had stopped with his ears pricked and his head tilted to one side. He was clearly listening to sounds that were inaudible to her.

"What is it, Waggit?" she asked. "What can you hear?"

"Shhhh," he said curtly.

Suddenly he started pulling her forward.

"Can you hear it?" he asked, but she could not.

They had only gone a short distance when he stopped once more.

"There it is again," he said. "You must be able to hear it now."

She strained her ears, turning her head back and forth, and then she did hear the faint sound of someone singing, fading in and out of the hum of the city. They moved forward in its direction until it became quite clear. It was a beautiful but sad song that drifted its sorrowful way over the bushes and the trees.

"It's her," said Waggit.

"Who?" inquired Felicia.

"The woman."

"Which woman?"

"The woman who abandoned me at the farm," said Waggit.

"Are you sure?" asked Felicia.

"I'd know that voice anywhere. She used to sing all the time when I lived with her."

"Let's go and see where she is," said Felicia, moving forward, but she had only gone two steps before she felt the leash pull tight in her hand. She turned to see Waggit sitting down on his haunches, his front legs splayed out, refusing to move.

"Come on, Waggit," she said. "She's not going to bite you. In fact, in the mood you're in now, you're more likely to bite her."

"I don't want to," said Waggit sulkily.

"Why not?" asked Felicia.

"I don't like her," replied Waggit. "I trusted her and she let me down."

"We don't know that," said Felicia. "There could be many reasons why she left you there. Wouldn't you like to know why it happened?"

Waggit had to admit that why she had just dumped him in that horrible place remained a complete mystery to him.

"I suppose," he said.

"She doesn't have to see you. You can hide in some bushes while I talk to her. Come on, it'll be worth it just to find out."

And so, still somewhat reluctantly, Waggit walked with Felicia in the direction of the sound. He knew exactly where the woman would be, in the same spot where the two of them had first met when he was just a puppy, and a hungry puppy at that. It was at the end of his first winter in the park, just as spring was starting to warm the air and humans were returning, relieved that the dark, cold days were almost over. She would come and sit on a rock, eat her lunch, and practice her songs. It had been her food rather than her music that had attracted Waggit, and she had shared it with him generously.

With some trepidation he approached the place where they had met and where he had been captured. Because he knew the location better than Felicia, he went first and brought them around to the side where a dense clump of bushes hid them from the woman's sight. He tensed as he saw her through the leaves. Watching her as she sang he felt such a mixture of emotions—anger, of course, because she'd abandoned him, but also, to his surprise, affection for her. He had warm memories of the life they had led: the soft bed she bought him and her scratching his stomach while he lay on it; the walks; the games in the park close to where they stood now; the two dogs who lived in the same building and who became his close friends. It may have lacked freedom, but living with her hadn't been bad at all.

"Stay here and don't twitch a whisker," Felicia whispered to him, and she moved out, around the bushes and toward the woman.

24

The Mystery Solved

The woman sat on the rock looking down at the sheet music on her lap. She was so absorbed in what she was doing that she failed to notice Felicia's approach.

"You sing beautifully," Felicia said.

The woman jumped, almost dropping the music.

"Oh, I'm sorry," she said. "I didn't hear you. Thank you."

"Are you a professional?" asked Felicia.

"Yes," replied the woman. "Whenever I can, I come

here to practice. It makes it a little easier on the neighbors."

"I always wanted to sing," Felicia said with a sigh, "but unfortunately I can't carry a tune in the proverbial bucket."

"I like it because if you're sad you can sing sad songs, and if you're happy, happy ones," said the woman.

"Then you must be sad today. That song is a very sad one," Felicia remarked.

The woman smiled wistfully.

"Well, maybe a little."

"I'm Felicia." She offered her hand.

"I'm Ruth," said the woman, shaking it.

Felicia sat next to Ruth, and, as she did, a runner went past with a panting dog in tow. When the dog saw the two women she tried to pull the runner toward them, without success.

"Cute dog," said Felicia. "I love dogs, don't you?"

Ruth paused before answering.

"I do," she finally replied, "but *they* can make you sad sometimes, too."

"That's true," said Felicia, "but they also give you a lot of love and joy. Do you have a dog?"

"I used to," answered Ruth sadly, "but I lost him,

and I haven't had the heart to get another."

"When you say you lost him," said Felicia, "do you mean he died?"

"No," replied Ruth, "I mean I really lost him. He disappeared." There was a pause, and then she said, "Do you have a dog?"

Felicia chuckled. "You wouldn't believe how many dogs I live with."

Ruth gave her a look that indicated she would believe almost anything of the strange-looking woman.

"How did your dog get lost?" Felicia asked.

"It's a long story."

"Tell me," Felicia persisted.

"Well, like I said," Ruth began, "I make my living as a singer. Usually I work around the city, but one day my agent called to say that a cruise ship was looking for a performer to replace someone who was sick, and could I leave straightaway. It was a three-month engagement, and the money was good, but I couldn't take my dog, so I had to quickly make arrangements for him to be looked after. I couldn't afford to put him in a kennel for all that time, and also I was worried that he would be scared there. He was a rescue dog, and the kennel would have looked like the pound where I got him. But I have a brother who has a big dairy farm upstate, and I thought three months in the fresh country air playing with the farm dogs would be good for Parker. Parker's what I called him."

"So what happened to him there?" asked Felicia.

"Well, you know," said Ruth, "I had forgotten that country people don't treat their dogs the way we do in the city. The farm dogs are working dogs, and they hardly ever go in the house. They live in the yard, and Parker was treated exactly the same as the others. I think my boy must have been very unhappy, because according to my brother he fought with the other dogs, which was something he never did in the park. In fact he was the friendliest dog you could imagine and loved to play. Anyway, one day he broke the chain that tethered him in the yard and got out and has never been seen since. I suppose he was run over or killed by coyotes or something horrible like that. I'll never forgive myself for doing that to him."

Her eyes were welling with tears as she told the story.

"I'm sorry," said Felicia. "I didn't mean to upset you. You know, dogs are remarkable survivors, and you can't assume that he's dead. You hear the most amazing stories of endurance—dogs that travel for hundreds of miles and turn up months after they go missing."

"I hope you're right," said Ruth, "but it's not knowing what happened to him that's the worst thing."

It was this last remark that caused Waggit so much pain later. He understood none of what had been said, of course, even though he overheard it but had to wait until the two women wished each other good-bye and Felicia retrieved him from behind the bush to find out what had happened. When she finished recounting the conversation, she looked at him with an "I-told-you-so" expression on her face.

Waggit himself was in a state of shock.

"I feel awful, Felicia," he finally said. "I was sure that she had just dumped me. The trouble is, when it's happened to you once, you're always half expecting it to happen again. What with Lug first, and now the woman—I seem to be wrong about everything."

"Well," said Felicia, "you can't do anything about Lug, but you could do something about Ruth."

"What?" asked Waggit.

"You could live with her again," said Felicia. "She'd take you back in a heartbeat."

Waggit thought for a minute.

"You know, Felicia," he said, "I can't do that. I realized when I came back to the park that I belong to the team. Part of me never really left it. For all its hardships and difficulties, this is my home, and these are my dogs. They're as much a part of me as my ears or my tail."

"In that case, my boy, you're going to have to be like everybody else and live with your mistakes. We all make 'em; I've made some whoppers, and at least in Ruth's case your mistake was a direct result of hers. That should be some consolation."

It should have been, but in fact it wasn't. Waggit felt bad for several days, knowing that he had hurt someone who cared for him, and that because of his own fears he had badly misjudged her. However his mind was soon taken up with other matters that would affect the future rather than the past.

The weather was getting cooler, clearly indicating that summer was over and autumn had arrived. The first frost hadn't yet happened, but there were mornings when the dogs' breath hung in the air like steam. It was a time of year that Waggit welcomed. He loved the combination of the early chill and the warmth of the sun later in the day. He and Lowdown were sitting with Gordo on a rock at the edge of the Deepwoods End watching some humans endlessly throw balls to one another, which, the dogs secretly thought, looked like it might be fun.

"This cool weather makes me feel so sort of bouncy," Waggit remarked.

"It makes me feel so sort of achy," replied Lowdown.

"It makes me feel hungry," grumbled Gordo.

"Anything makes you feel hungry," said Lowdown.

Just then Felicia joined them. She was hunched up and rubbing the tops of her arms, trying to get warm.

"Wow," she said. "It's a little chilly today."

"We was just remarking on the same thing," said Lowdown. "Apparently it makes Mr. Activity here full of bounce."

"It makes me full of dread," Felicia remarked. "I can't take it."

"Me neither," agreed Lowdown. "My old bones throb something terrible in the cold."

"I have to find a warmer place than here to live during the Long Cold," said Felicia.

"Like the flutters, you mean?" asked Gordo.

"I suppose, in a way," replied Felicia. "Like them I shall have to leave you all, at least until next year."

"Where will you go?" asked Waggit.

"Somewhere south of here," said Felicia. "I'm not exactly sure where."

"Where's south?" asked Gordo.

Felicia pointed in the direction of the skyscrapers at the far end of the park.

"The Skyline End?" said Gordo, incredulously. "The Skyline End ain't any warmer than the Deepwoods. In fact most of the time it's a lot windier."

"No, Gordo." Felicia smiled. "Somewhere much farther in that direction than the Skyline End. Farther even than the journey that Waggit and I took together."

There was silence as the three dogs contemplated the possibility of such a monumental expedition.

"When—um—when do you think you might leave?" asked Waggit hesitantly.

"Quite soon," said Felicia. "I think I might hit the road tomorrow."

A gloom fell over the three dogs. Felicia leaving, and being without her help and wise advice, not to mention the occasional feasts that she put on, would cause an empty space in the team that would be impossible to fill. There wasn't one dog who had a bad word to say about her now, and they all recognized that she was an exceptional human being, one like they would never meet again; she had subtly altered the way they—even Tazar—felt about "Uprights."

"We're going to miss you," said Waggit.

"Oh, I'll be back," Felicia assured him. "You don't think I'm going to give up all the friends I've made here, do you? As soon as it gets warm you'll see me crashing through the woods again."

"I believe you will," agreed Lowdown, "and I hope I'm here to see it, but that don't mean we ain't going to miss you in the meantime."

"And I will miss you," said Felicia, "and I'm sure you'll be here when I return. A tough, leathery old character like you is hard to get rid of. Well, I must be off. I've got to pop into town to get some things for the journey."

Gordo's ears pricked up.

"No, Gordo," she said. "Upright things—nothing you'd be interested in."

She headed toward the Skyline End, and as she did

the three dogs watched her tall, lanky body stride away.

"I can't believe she's leaving," Waggit said with a sigh.

"Well, to be fair," Lowdown pointed out, "she always said she would. We knew this was just temporary for her."

"I know," agreed Waggit, "but I hoped she would change her mind."

"I thought she liked us," said Gordo mournfully.

"She does," said Lowdown. "Just because she's leaving don't mean she ain't our friend no more."

The three dogs left their rock to bring the bad news to the rest of the team. They found most of its members enjoying the sun in the meadow by the entrance to the pipe. The reaction to Felicia leaving was the same: real sadness edged with a tinge of disbelief. As he heard them talk about her, Waggit realized that the reason they were so fond of her was that they saw in her the qualities, real or imaginary, that they most valued in themselves. Alicia thought she was classy; Magica saw her as a caring, nurturing person; Cal and Raz thought she was fun; Tazar valued her ability to think strategically; Alona recognized her as a true outsider, one who followed her own path; Gruff thought she was one of the few creatures who really understood his problems and sympathized with him. Waggit simply thought of her as a loyal friend, whose guidance he would miss.

"We should do something so she knows how sad we are to see her go," said Magica.

Everyone murmured that this was a good idea, but nobody could work out what would be suitable.

"Maybe we could hunt her a hopper," said Gordo, "and let her have it all without sharing."

In Gordo's mind there was no higher act of gener-osity.

"Nah," said Raz, "that ain't going to work. Felicia only likes her food burned, and we don't know how to do fire."

"Which is just as well," said Gruff, "'cause if you did you'd probably burn the whole park down, and then where would we be?"

"Maybe we could all groom her," suggested Alicia.

"How about we play a really good game with her?" asked Cal.

The ideas came and went, each of them impractical or inappropriate, until Tazar cleared his throat.

"None of these is going to work," he said, "because they're all what *you* want to do. What we need to do is to show her the way the whole team feels about her, and the best way to do that is to tell her. Since Waggit was the one who brought her to us, he should be the one to do it."

And so it was decided that at the evening meal they would gather around Felicia, and Waggit would speak on their behalf and try to make her realize how important she had become to all the dogs and how they hoped that she would be back as soon as the warm weather returned.

25

A Friend's Good-bye

That afternoon, as luck would have it, Cal and Raz found a box that contained an almost complete pizza. They came across it farther from the Deepwoods than they usually went and had to drag their prize back to the pipe. This, they insisted, was to be a farewell gift for Felicia, and both of them guarded it until the evening meal, growling ferociously whenever anyone came close. Felicia seemed delighted with the offering when it was presented to her, although as Gordo noted, she left most of it.

"I guess that's why she stays so thin," he later confided to Waggit.

It was a pleasant meal, despite an edge of sadness. In the conversations that took place between mouthfuls, they reminisced about Felicia and the time that she had spent in the park. Despite her promises to return when the weather got warmer, it was difficult for the dogs to think that far ahead, living on a day-to-day basis as they did. As the meal was winding down, lips were being smacked, and yawns were beginning to be yawned, Tazar got up and cleared his throat.

"Lady Felicia," he began when he had their attention, "this meal was the last we will enjoy with you for some time. You have brought much pleasure to our team in the months you have been with us, but tonight there's more sorrow than joy because you are leaving. I never thought I'd say this about an Upright, but we will miss you. We wanted to get you something to remember us by, but we're just dogs, and poor ones at that. What we have is of no use to you. The only thing we can give you is what we most value: the love we have for one another, and that we give you wholeheartedly. I'm not one for long speeches; I'm more a dog of action." There were smothered snorts and giggles at this point. "So I'm going to let one who speaks better than I tell you how we feel about you."

He nodded to Waggit, who got to his feet.

"Felicia," said Waggit, "I know if it wasn't for you I wouldn't be standing here tonight, and I wouldn't be reunited with my family, these dogs. You saved my life, but you not only saved my life, you made it better. You told me that it was okay if I wasn't perfect, that it's only canine to get angry or jealous. But you also showed me that it's not okay if I don't *try* to be the best I can, that I have to try to be loving and compassionate and brave, even if I don't think I am. You made me a better team member because of it. When we were talking about what to do tonight the whole team spoke about the way they felt about you. Some mentioned how wise you are, and others how caring, but the one thing everyone said was that you seem like a dog, and a team dog at that. No Upright was ever given such a compliment, but you earned it. So now you are officially a Tazarian, and every time you're in the park we will protect you and care for you. I don't know how many risings will pass before we see you again, but I know we will. Once you're a Tazarian you're always a Tazarian. You'll always come back."

As he finished his speech the team erupted in a roar of yelps, barks, and howls, scaring the life out of a couple of Uprights who had braved the darkness of the woods, strolling hand in hand to get some peace and quiet. For her part Felicia was in tears, unable to speak, but still able to stroke, kiss, and tickle each one of them under the chin before they turned in for the night.

She spent the first part of the following day folding her tent, checking the contents of her backpack, putting new laces in her boots, then rechecking the backpack and fiddling with the tent and the sleeping bag that were attached to it. The dogs realized that she was putting off leaving, but finally she sighed, stood up, and heaved the pack onto her back, adjusting the straps around her shoulders. She turned to look at the mournful faces watching her.

"Time to go," she said simply, and strode off into the woods in the direction of the Skyline End that the dogs now knew was south.

"Bye, Felicia."

"Come back soon."

"Don't forget us."

She didn't turn around, but marched off and soon

disappeared into the trees.

"Well, I suppose that's the last we'll see of her," grumbled Gruff.

"No, she'll be back sometime," Lowdown assured him.

"I hope so," said Magica. "What makes you so sure she will?"

"I feel it in my old bones."

"Oh, you and your bones," shrieked Alicia. "You feel everything in your bones—what the weather's gonna be, where the Ruzelas are, who ain't telling the truth. You got the most overworked bones of any dog I know."

"Yeah," said Lowdown, "and when have they been wrong?"

This silenced Alicia and the rest of the team, because nobody could remember a time when they couldn't rely on Lowdown to accurately predict things, and his bones were as good an explanation for this ability as anything. In fact the only sound that could be heard was Tazar muttering to himself.

"I've never met one like her before, that's for sure, and I don't think I'm ever likely to again."

But however sorry you are to see someone go,

and however much you miss them, life has to go on; it's a matter of survival. Food had to be hunted, sentries posted, coats groomed, and all the other tasks that made up life in the park had to be carried out. Not that anyone forgot Felicia, but as the days passed she became just one of the things they thought about, mostly when some part of the park reminded them of something she had done there. The little stone monument to Lug that she had erected over his grave flooded them with memories every time they passed it. Some dogs avoided going that way if they could.

Tazar was still having difficulty coming to terms with the defection of his son to the enemy team, and the other dogs feared he never would. The snippets of information that he got about the boy through the park grapevine didn't help either. Rumor had it that Olang hadn't just joined Tashi's old team but was now leading it. One of the loners reported that he had changed its name from the Tashinis to the Olangsters (or Olangster's Gangsters as Lowdown immediately renamed them) and was recruiting new members wherever he could. In order to do this he was using some of the larger, tougher dogs on his team to "persuade" unfortunate loners or newly abandoned animals to become part of the group. Now that he was without the oversight of his father, his bullying knew no bounds.

"I don't get it," Tazar said to Waggit after hearing another report of his wayward son's activities. "I still don't understand why he went against me. I cared for him, I gave him all a puppy could need, and I was grooming him to take over as leader when I'm no longer able to carry out my duties. He had everything he could want."

"Oftentimes dogs have to make their own mistakes, to find things out for themselves," said Lowdown, who had been listening to the conversation. He might have added, "especially when they have domineering parents," but he didn't.

"No," Waggit assured Tazar, "it was me. For some reason he felt threatened by me being here. He felt you were paying me too much attention, and that you didn't respect him as much as he wanted you to."

"I heard," Tazar said, "that he's telling dogs that the reason he left the team was that I'm too old to lead, that I'm past it."

He paused for a moment, a mournful look on his usually proud face.

"I sometimes wonder if he's right," Tazar continued.

"Maybe I am too old and too set in my ways. Perhaps I should've stepped aside and let him take over."

Waggit looked at this exceptional dog, who may have had a few gray hairs around his muzzle but who was physically fit, strong, and in the prime of his life. He worried that Olang's treachery would paralyze Tazar's ability to lead the team. One of the things that the Tazarians liked about their chief was the fact that he made decisions, took action. If he was wrong he always admitted it, but he did not allow past mistakes to prevent him from being decisive in the future. This self-doubt and self-pity were new and ominous. As if to confirm his fears, Tazar let out a monumental sigh and without a word to the other two, loped off into the woods, his magnificent tail drooping and his ears down.

"He's in bad shape, isn't he?" asked Waggit.

"Yeah," replied Lowdown. "He's taking this real hard."

"What will happen if it stops him from being our leader?"

"Why, you'll take over," said Lowdown, as if this were obvious.

"Me?" exclaimed Waggit. "Me? I told you before, I can't lead the team."

"You," Lowdown insisted. "Yes, you. Why can't you lead the team?"

"I'm too young, for one thing," Waggit said.

"Do me a favor," said Lowdown. "The next time you're by the Bigwater take a look at your reflection. Like the rest of us, my friend, you're getting older by the minute. You ain't as young as you seem to think you are."

"But I've never done any leading," protested Waggit. "I wouldn't know how."

"Yes, you have," said Lowdown. "For one thing you led Lug here."

"Yes," said Waggit, "to his death."

"That's beside the point," said Lowdown. "The fact of the matter is that he followed you here, and he looked up to you and respected you, as do the rest of the team, I might add. Besides which Tazar would expect you to take over if anything happened to him. Why do you think he was so glad to see you back? It wasn't 'cause you're so pretty, 'cause you ain't. Nah, I've got a suspicion that deep in the back of his mind he had an inkling all along that Olang wasn't up to it. That's why you turning up was perfect timing. You was his fallback."

"Well!" was all Waggit could think to say, and he sat down and scratched behind his left ear with his back leg, a sure sign that he was thinking deeply about something. He had honestly never thought of himself leading the team, and although the idea of it filled him with pride, it was also very scary. He barely felt capable of looking after himself, never mind all of his friends. He was mulling over these new ideas when there was a sudden crashing sound and the present leader came barreling through the woods. He had clearly recovered from his recent doldrums and was once again very much in charge.

"Waggit, I need you. Come with me," he commanded.

Waggit, relieved to resume following rather than leading, was quickly on his feet and pursuing Tazar's plumed black tail, which was once again firmly held high.

26
Puppies in Distress

Waggit chased Tazar through brush and woods, across open paths and over rocks that jutted out high over the road running inside the park that the dogs called the rollerway. For a dog who thought he was too old to lead the team, Tazar was almost too fast and agile for Waggit to keep up with him. He finally stopped next to an ancient, grizzled dog who Waggit recognized as a loner living in this part of the Deepwoods. The dogs had stopped at a vantage point from which they could see the road beneath them and a crowd of humans gathered around three cars. It seemed that the rear two had smashed into the front one when it pulled up sharply. A group of humans was clustered around the front car, and some kind of a commotion was going on. The loner nodded to Tazar.

"She ran straight out in front of the roller," he said, as if answering an unasked question.

"Is she dead?" asked Tazar.

"She ain't," said the old loner, "but she might as well be. They've catched her and they'll never let her go now, 'specially as they've bust their precious rollers. What's even worse is she's got two youngsters, that was born only a few risings ago."

"Are they down there?" asked Tazar.

"Nah, she's got a spot on the other side of Farpoint Hill. They're probably over there, but they're real young. Without her they're as good as dead already," he said glumly.

"You loners are so pessimistic," cried Tazar. "Those puppies may be in a bad situation, but they're not dead yet and won't be if I can help it."

So with the scent of adventure in his nostrils Tazar led Waggit toward the area that the dogs called Farpoint Hill. This was in the far northeastern section of the park and was favored by loners because few humans ever climbed its slopes, and yet it was close to the garbage cans lining the sidewalk at the edge of the park. These provided a reliable source of food, even if their contents were often somewhat strange.

The two dogs had a general idea as to where the pups were likely to be. When they got to the area, however, it was clear why humans didn't visit this part of the park much. The sides of the hill were quite steep and heavily covered in brush and trees. The few paths that wound around were overgrown or blocked by fallen branches. It was certainly a good spot to hide a young family from predators, both human and animal. Waggit and Tazar split up, each taking a section, and as methodically as possible began to search for the orphaned puppies.

Because the hill provided sanctuary to many animals, not just to dogs, Waggit found it difficult to get a scent of the two they were looking for. The area was home to raccoons, squirrels, skunks, mice, rats, and any number of other creatures, each of which had its own smell, and each of which confused Waggit's sensitive nose. In the end it wasn't his nose that found the puppies but Tazar's ears. He picked up the faint sound of crying, almost like the mewling of a kitten. The sound finally led him to a cluster of tree roots where two tiny puppies lay. One was quieter than the other, who appeared to be much stronger. Very gently Waggit and Tazar each lifted one up, holding them in their mouths and clamping their teeth on the loose skin at the back of the puppies' tiny necks. They then started back in the direction of the pipe, moving carefully through the thick foliage. Both puppies squealed as they were carried along, the louder one wriggling so hard that Tazar found it difficult to keep her firmly in his mouth without hurting her.

When they got to the foot of the hill they had to hide for several minutes, waiting for a moment when their route was free of both pedestrians and cars. They finally cleared the road and made their way back up the rocks and across the woods to the pipe.

The first dog to greet them when they arrived was Magica. Of the three females on the team, she was the only one who showed any maternal instincts. Alicia's attitude about puppies was that they were noisy, messy, and, even worse, took attention away from her. While Alona enjoyed the company of young dogs, and had played extensively with Little One and Little Two when they were small, she lacked the self-confidence to take charge of them in the way that was completely natural for Magica.

"Oh my, oh my," Magica said, "those poor young things. Where did they come from?"

Tazar and Waggit gently put the two babies down on the ground, where they walked awkwardly around, bumping into each other and making little crying sounds.

"They belong to a loner," said Tazar, "who was involved in some nonsense with three rollers near Farpoint Hill, and she got captured by the Uprights. So we rescued them."

"Bless you for that," said Magica at the same time that Alicia said, "Whadja bring 'em back here for? We can't do anything for 'em. They're way too young."

The sad fact of the matter was that Alicia was right, as they found out when they tried to feed the puppies some food that Magica had chewed until it was as soft as she could make it. They were simply too tiny to be able to consume it. The best the dogs could do was to get them to drink a little water by taking a mouthful themselves and then dripping it into their open mouths. But clearly this was only going to keep them alive for so long.

"They need milk," said Magica.

"Well, we don't have any," said Tazar, "and where in the park we'd get some I don't know."

"Felicia would know if she was here," said Waggit.

"Well, she's not," Tazar responded sharply, "so that doesn't help."

"There might be some at the feeder," said Gordo. "They have it there in little boxes. I know 'cause one of the Uprights what works there threw one at me one time when I was trying to get some food, and it burst and went all over me. It was white stuff, so I think it was milk."

"It's worth a try," said Tazar, "but it's best if we wait till dark when they put out all the stuff they don't want."

The Upright feeder was a restaurant in the park that had once been part of Tashi's realm. Since his team's capture it had become the province of all of the dogs in the park and was a constant and reliable source of food, most of it too spoiled to be served to customers but perfectly acceptable to a hungry animal.

Cal, Raz, Tazar, and Waggit set out as soon as darkness fell and made their way slowly and carefully down to the place by the lake where the restaurant was located. Tazar said that Cal should be the one to make the snatch if the opportunity presented itself. He wasn't quite as fast as Waggit, but he was fast enough, and he had the added advantage of a dark coat that would be less noticeable at night.

After an uneventful journey they arrived at their destination and hid in some bushes that gave them a clear view of the back door that led straight into the kitchens. It was still too early in the evening for the waste to be thrown into the Dumpsters, so they settled down to wait. They watched the comings and goings of the taxis and black limousines as well as the horse-drawn carriages that worked in this part of the park. After an hour or two the doors to the kitchen opened and a man in a stained white apron came out, staggering under the weight of a large black plastic bag that he threw into one of several Dumpsters near the door. He went back in, and shortly afterward came out with a blue plastic crate that was half filled with several tall cardboard boxes. He placed the crate on the ground beside a Dumpster.

"That's them," said Raz. "Them's the boxes what Gordo was talking about."

They waited to see what the man would do next. He didn't go back into the kitchen but sat down and lit a cigarette. The dogs thought it mystifying that humans sometimes put white sticks in their mouths and then set them on fire, but so much of what Uprights did was puzzling that they didn't try to work it out. It wasn't his smoking that bothered them, however, as much as the fact that he remained outside and close to the crate containing their prize.

"Let's wait and see if he moves," said Tazar. "He can't stay there all night."

The man puffed on his cigarette in a leisurely manner, stretched, yawned, looked around, and appeared to be perfectly happy, with no desire to return to work at all. After several minutes had passed without any indication that the man was about to go back inside, Cal began to get restless.

"You see that box what's by itself?" he said. "I think I could snatch it quick enough that he couldn't get me. It's worth a try."

The other dogs had noticed that one of the cartons was away from the others in a corner of the crate, and that the corner was the closest to the dogs and the farthest from the man.

"It's not worth the risk," said Tazar. "Let's wait a little longer."

"Nah, I think I can do it," said Cal, but before he could sprint off fate took control.

"Hold it," hissed Tazar. "Look!"

Making their way through the bushes that edged the restaurant the Tazarians could see another group of dogs. As they broke cover they became identifiable.

"It's Tashi's team," said Raz. "I mean—Olang's team."

Waggit saw Tazar flinch at the mention of Olang's name. Now that they were in open ground the motley group of animals that made up the Olangsters spread out and moved toward the Dumpsters. Olang himself was not among the front-line troops but standing back on a nearby hill watching the action. They made no attempt to conceal themselves but crept forward low to the ground, their fangs bared, ready to attack. When the restaurant worker saw them advancing toward him he threw away his cigarette and fled back into the building.

At this point the dogs started to rip open the black plastic bags of garbage. Before they could make off with any of the contents the man returned with another, both armed with brooms. They yelled at the dogs, swinging at them with their improvised weapons. Immediately the Olangsters turned tail and fled back in the direction they had come, much to Olang's fury as he barked orders to them that were completely ignored. Emboldened by their success the two men pursued the fleeing animals into the woods.

"Go now," Tazar yelled at Cal, who needed no further persuasion.

At full speed he raced toward the crate and clamped his jaw around the single carton. He pulled, but it would not budge, and so he shook it fiercely, as he would have done with any other prey. This released it, and just in time, for the two men were now returning, brooms at the ready.

"There's another one," one of them cried.

"Let's get him," said the other, and they started running in Cal's direction. But the dog now had his prize and was on his way back to his waiting comrades. There wasn't a human being alive that could outrun Cal, and certainly not these two, whose years of employment in the restaurant business were reflected in their waistlines. The best they could do was stand puffing heavily and shaking their brooms at Cal's departing figure.

"Well done," Tazar congratulated Cal upon his return. "Now let's get it to the youngsters."

The four of them started the journey back to the pipe. When they got there they found Magica pacing up and down, a worried look on her face.

"Oh, thank goodness you got it," she said when she saw the carton. "These two have been crying the whole time you were away."

Indeed they could all hear the pathetic sound of whimpering coming from the hungry puppies, but when they attempted to open the carton, none of them knew how to do it. Waggit tried holding it in between his front paws and pulling on the top with his teeth, but all that achieved was a waxy taste in his mouth. Little One and Little Two took a corner each and pulled in opposite directions, and while that was great fun, it had little effect on the sealed top. Then Gordo stepped forward with the authority of one who had never been beaten by food packaging.

"Here, let me have a go," he said in a tone of voice indicating that it was time to get serious. He then pulled back his lip, and using his huge, curved canine punched a hole on one side of the carton top.

"Good going, Gordo," said Tazar.

"No, wait," said Gordo, "you need another hole on the other side, otherwise nothing'll come out."

He then repeated the process, but made a face as he tasted the contents.

"Yuck," he spluttered, "it's awful."

"Don't worry," said Magica. "It'll taste great to the kids."

Unfortunately she was soon proven wrong. She took the carton in her mouth and went over to the weaker of the two. Both puppies had their mouths open, desperate for food, and she tilted it toward the tiny creatures. Nothing happened. There was no flow of white liquid that would nourish and sustain them. She shook the carton with her head, and after the third or fourth shake out came a large, congealed glob. The milk was sour.

27

Waggit Makes Amends

Nobody slept well that night, what with the puppies mewling as their hunger got worse, and Magica fussing around them, distressed by their distress. The situation wasn't helped by Alicia and Gruff complaining that they couldn't get a wink of sleep and thereby preventing anyone else from doing so. All in all, the pipe was not a restful place, and Waggit was glad when dawn finally came and he could leave its confines. He wandered over to Lowdown's tree to find the old fellow painfully stretching in front of it.

"Oooh," he complained, "this gets harder and harder every day. I sometimes wonder why I bother to get up."

"Well," said Waggit, "I wonder why I bothered to go to bed last night."

He explained what the night had been like, and his worry about the puppies, who at this moment were only existing on whatever water could be dripped into their mouths. The older dog lay down, scratched behind his ears, and sighed.

"You know," he said, "Tazar don't want to hear this, but there's times when only an Upright can solve a situation, and this is one of them. The problem is that he's right when he says you can't trust 'em. That was why it was so good to have Felicia around; you got the best of both worlds with her. No, the fact of the matter is, those two youngsters is going to die, and there ain't a thing we can do about it. It's a crying shame."

Waggit didn't want to believe this. There must be a way of saving the two young lives if only he could think of it. He said good-bye to Lowdown and wandered off into the woods, pondering the dilemma and trying to think of a solution.

Later that morning he was still mulling the situation

over in his mind when he heard a familiar sound. He was near the Risingside, close to the place where the woman practiced her songs, and it was her voice that he heard now. Then it struck him like a falling rock— here was the answer to their problems. She was the Upright who could save the puppies, if he could only get them to her without revealing himself.

He raced back to the pipe. When he got there he found several of the dogs, including Tazar, grouped around the youngsters, looks of concern on their faces. The two babies were already weaker. One no longer even cried but just lay on the ground with a dull look in his eyes. Waggit explained his idea to the group, but Tazar would have none of it.

"No," he said. "I'm not going to be party to condemning two dogs to the life of a petulant. It's slavery, that's what it is, just slavery. Better to die free in the park than that."

"Well, I have to tell you," said Waggit, "that when I lived with her it was pretty comfortable slavery."

"But you still came back to us," said Tazar, "and why? Because she abandoned you, because Uprights can't be trusted and can't be relied upon."

"No, she didn't," said Waggit. "I thought she did,

but all she actually did was not think straight, and she's probably learned her lesson. She won't do that again."

But it was the puppies themselves who finally swayed Tazar. The stronger of the two started to cry again, and when the big black dog put his face close to her she began to lick his nose, begging for food. Seeing this Magica decided to add her considerable powers of persuasion.

"Look at them, Tazar," she said. "How can you condemn them to a horrible and painful death when they could be saved? Hasn't there been enough death around here without adding two innocent souls to those who have already gone? Give them a chance to live."

Tazar knew when he was beaten, and so shortly afterward Waggit and Magica headed toward the spot where the woman sang, each with a puppy in his or her mouth. When they got to the bushes, they crouched low and edged as close as they could go without being seen. Gently putting the young dogs on the ground they pushed them toward the woman. But the more they pushed, the more the puppies came back to them. Even the weaker one was crying now, both of them scared at being separated from the older animals.

The woman was singing loudly, and so couldn't

hear what was happening just a few feet in front of her. Waggit indicated to Magica that she should move back. He then corralled the puppies into a little hollow in the ground near the edge of the bushes closest to the woman. He kept them there with his paws while she sang, and when she paused for a moment, he made a crying sound like the noise the baby dogs made, only much louder. The woman turned her head in the direction of the sound. Waggit held his breath. He wanted her to hear him, but he certainly didn't want her to find him.

"Hello," said the woman. "Who's there?"

Waggit made the sound again and then moved back to the far side of the bushes, the back part of his body in open ground. He saw the woman part the lower branches of the shrubs.

"Oh my," she said, sounding remarkably like Magica, "where did you two come from? Oh, you poor things."

Waggit held his breath and didn't move a whisker, willing the woman to pick up the two tiny creatures. He did not have to wait long for his prayer to be answered. She leaned forward and gently lifted first one and then the other away from the bushes and held them up to look at them. Both puppies cried at this strange creature holding them, which made her cuddle them more.

"Oh no," said the woman. "What am I doing? Are you going to break my heart as well?"

She looked down at them.

"Oh well," she said with a sigh. "I'd better take you to the vet and find out what on earth I can feed you."

Waggit, who understood none of the words, had a perfect comprehension of her body language, and he knew that the dogs would be in good hands.

"Did she take them?" asked Magica, who had been too far away to see.

"She did," said Waggit. "All is well."

The two of them walked back to the pipe, light in both heart and step.

Later that night as Waggit lay outside under the stars before taking his place next to the other dogs, he thought about all the things that had happened to him since escaping from the farm. He thought about Felicia and Lug, and how glad he was that Lowdown was still around, and Tazar and Olang, and the terrible fight with Tashi, and the puppies and the woman. He was still a young dog, almost a puppy himself, but he felt old beyond his years. So much had happened in such a short period of time. He had learned about survival and friendship, and loyalty and bravery through overcoming fear. He had also come to understand that the world was not always the friendly place he would like it to be. There were bad dogs like Olang and Tashi, and bad humans like the men at the bar, and these you had to stand up to, even though it was scary and dangerous.

Lug's death still weighed heavily on him, but in some strange way that he didn't fully understand, saving the lives of the two puppies made up for the guilt he felt over the way he had treated the pit bull. It somehow restored the balance, two lives saved for one lost. It also made him feel better about misjudging the woman, and he knew that the two little ones would be safe with her. What *he* had learned was that both humans and dogs are often different from the way they first seem, and to judge too quickly was often to be wrong. It was a lesson he would try to live by.

He got up, stretched, yawned, and hopped lightly into the entry to the pipe. The other Tazarians were already there, and he trod as carefully as he could to get past the sleeping bodies, but, as always, it was very dark inside. Of course, the one dog he would tread on with all his weight was Gruff, who growled in a low, deep voice:

"It's okay, Waggit, don't mind me. I've got three other legs, so I probably won't miss the use of this one."

Waggit apologized quietly and finally made it to his place next to Cal and Raz. He lay down, comforted by the sound of their breathing and the warmth of their bodies.

"Good night, Cal. Good night, Raz."

"Sleep well, Waggit," said Raz. "See you in the rising."

GLOSSARY

Bad water: Gasoline

Bigwater: The reservoir

The Cold White: Snow

Curlytails: Squirrels

Deepwater: The lake

Deepwoods End: The north end of the park

Eyes and ears: Sentry duty

Feeder: Restaurant

Flutters: Birds

Goldenside: The West side of the park

The Great Unknown: The dog pound

Half-Roller: Bicycle

Hoppers: Rabbits

Loners: Dogs with no team

The Long Cold: Winter

Longlegs: Horses

Luggers: Carriages pulled by horses

Nibblers: Mice

Petulants: Pet dogs

Realm: Area of the park that is the domain of a team

Rising: Day

Risingside: The East side of the park

Rollers: Cars

Rollerway: Road going through the park

Ruzelas: Anyone in authority—rangers, police, etc.

Scurries: Rats

Silver claws: Knives

Skurdie: A homeless person in the park

Skyline End: The south end of the park

Stoners: Teenage boys

Uprights: Human beings